Ooh, What Are All These Pains!

A Novel and a Historical Recap

Dr Raafat Khalaf

Dedication

To Samia

Introduction

The title of this novel is taken from a phrase in the book "The Wonders of Antiquities in Biographies and News" by the great 18th-century historian al-Jabarti. Al-Jabarti wrote that during the Cairenes' revolt against the French army, they shouted, "Ya Salaam of these alaam", meaning "Ooh, what are all these pains" when Napoleon Bonaparte's bombs rained down upon them, bombs they had never seen before! Al-Jabarti may have chosen the word "Ya Salam" only to conform with the rhyme of the assonance, yet he succeeded in conveying the people's astonishment and anguish with striking clarity.

The world does not need a new book on the French campaign against Egypt and the Levant at the beginning of the nineteenth century. Much has been written about it in French, English, and Arabic. More books have been written about Napoleon Bonaparte than any other leader in world history. Yet the exploration of human motives and emotions is endless, and the lived experiences of ordinary people still hold stories worth telling.

This novel offers a narrative interpretation of the first year of the campaign, following the daily lives of Egyptians, French, and English individuals who endured those turbulent events. Amid violence and destruction, it weaves a love story that unfolds as Egypt is thrust into the heart of the struggle between the two great powers of the eighteenth century: England and France.

History has two faces: the face shaped by events and their leaders, and the face reflected in the lives of ordinary people whom history books often overlook. In this novel, the major events and historical figures are presented as they appear in original sources, while the experiences of ordinary people are imagined—crafted to reveal the emotional truths that official records leave unsaid. The historical sources on which I relied include the writings of al-Jabarti and Nicola Turc, Napoleon's memoirs, official French campaign record, letters from French soldiers and officers to their families in France, documents from British National Archives, and accounts by European travellers who visited Egypt around the time of the campaign.

Perhaps the most important lesson we learn from history is that we do not learn from history. And so history repeats itself. The events born of human diversity, cultural difference, and the conflicts and suffering that follow are the same stories retold across the ages. Circumstances change, but human nature and human emotion remain constant everywhere and throughout time.

Al-Jabarti's renowned work stands as a model of scholarly integrity and precision. Most scholars consider his account highly reliable and frequently cite it as a trusted source. Although he occasionally expresses personal feelings rooted in his strong religious identity and pride in Islam, he nonetheless describes events with the objectivity of a dedicated academic. I have included excerpts from his writings throughout this novel.

I wish to pay tribute to al-Jabarti here. Reading his work reveals not only the events of that period in Egypt's history but also the character of the man himself—sensitive, perceptive, and deeply attuned to the emotions of the people he wrote about. His unwavering commitment to truth, his refusal to flatter rulers or yield to pressure to alter historical facts, cost him dearly. Yet he left future generations a priceless and honest record.

Dr Raafat Khalaf

United Kingdom

Contents

It happened on 2nd July 1798   8

It happened on 23rd July 1798   75

It happened on 1st August 1798   95

It happened in September 1798   122

It happened on 21st October 1798   144

It happened in December 1798   163

It happened in January 1799   195

It happened in February 1799   218

It happened in May 1799   243

It happened in June 1799   264

It happened in July 1799   283

It happened in August 1799   303

"Year thirteen, two hundred and one thousand (Hijri year)

The first of the years of the great epics and the grave events,

The coming cataclysms, the enormous calamities,

Evils multiply, and things tandem

And the succession of tribulations and the imbalance of time,

and the reflection of the printed and the inversion of the subject,

And the succession of horrors, and the difference of conditions,

the corruption of the measures, the occurrence of destruction,

And the generality of devastation and the straining of causes,

And your God would never destroy a village if its people were reformists".

Abdul Rahman Bin Hassan al-Jabarti

From the book "The Marvelous Compositions of Biographies and News."

Cairo 1798

It happened on 2nd July 1798

Al-Sanadikya district, Cairo

As usual, the friends gathered around shisha, coffee cups, and cups of cinnamon drink with added crushed hazelnuts in the early evening, but this time a lot of anxiety, anticipation, and confusion dominated their gathering. A few days ago, the speeding horses of messengers came with an urgent message from Sayyid Muhammad Kurayyim, the governor of Alexandria, with the news of the arrival of a fleet of English ships in the seaport. This spread tension and fear of a new Crusader invasion. And then came the news of the departure of the English ships to reassure and relieve the anxiety of the masses. But it did not take much time before the speeding horses arrived again from Alexandria, this time, with news of the arrival of French ships. It was so vast a fleet that no one could see where their numbers ended. All of a sudden, the inhabitants of Alexandria were confronted with enormous numbers of French soldiers. Like locusts, they spread everywhere, to occupy the city.

The friends were a group of wealthy and elite Cairenes who were not of the same religious affiliation but had a friendship that stretched back many years. They had a lot of insider knowledge and much influence on events due to their close ties over the years with Mameluke princes, Ulema (Islamic scholars) and Turkish rulers. Their almost daily evening gatherings were the source of comfort and peace in their lives. They were always eager to come to it, prevented only by reasons of travel or illness. Daytime in al-Sanadikya is full of banging, noise, bustle and shouting from the many workshops in the neighbourhood, but the gathering place, in the back garden of the large house of Haj Mustafa brought joy and peace in the evening when there was silence. The men sat on a balcony facing the garden under a vine-covered pergola, surrounded by ivy and many mint, basil and jasmine bushes that added a beautiful fragrance to the place. In their usual conversation, they liked to exchange views on what was happening in Cairo and Egypt. Each of them liked to talk about the events of their day and what they intended to do, and each of them talked about the news of their children and grandchildren. They all knew everything about each other, and the conversation was not without a sense of humour. Sarcastic remarks and jokes were directed at events and people they met during the day, and even a vendor, barber or Sakka (a man sells clear fresh water) could not escape their ridicule. They also directed their sarcastic remarks towards each other. Then, their loud laughs and guffaws penetrated the doors and walls and broke the evening silence in the quiet lane.

Their usual loud laughter was not heard the evening following the news of the invasion. They learned that the French chief had issued a communiqué, many copies of which were distributed in Alexandria and had now arrived in Cairo. Haj Mustafa got one of them that everyone read carefully before they began talking:

> 'No one knows what the days will hold. The country of Egypt has not faced an external invasion for hundreds of years, and the Franks have never dared to approach the Sultan's land before.'
>
> 'I do not believe a single word of that communiqué. If the Franks really came with the approval of the Sultan, then why do we not see with them any correspondence from him to prove this?'

'The infidel chief of the Franks is trying to win people over with the Qur'an. Who believes that Franks are Muslims?'

'I agree; but, the communiqué gives me some reassurance. No one knows precisely what the true intentions of the Franks are, but at least it does not appear to be an evil omen in this communiqué.'

'Europe has changed a lot from what the Mameluke princes know. They do not even know what is happening in the world around them, so perhaps the arrival of the English fleet before the French fleet gave them a clue.'

'What might be this clue?'

'That the Franks' enemy is the English, not the Sultan in Istanbul.'

'The days will reveal what they are up to. We must prepare for difficult days ahead.'

'It is necessary to confront the Franks, and the Mameluke princes can crush them, and protect the people. No one doubts that.'

'The Sultan's army is far away, and the princes are all we have for defence. Despite what we see from the princes of oppression and brutality, no one doubts their courage and skill in chivalry and fighting.'

'Do not underestimate the Franks; they are now different from the Franks defeated by the Princes centuries ago.'

As usual, their opinions on current affairs conflicted; they argued for a time but all agreed that they would face difficult times ahead and should prepare for them as best they could. Everyone went home with fear, anxiety and confusion all over them.

Kasr Al-Aini, Cairo

The worrying news arrived from Alexandria and Rashid that the countless ships of the French fleet had docked in the Gulf of Abu Qir and that large numbers of French soldiers had taken charge of both cities, so the members of the Diwan had been summoned in a hurry to attend an emergency session at the palace of al-Aini or Kasr al-Aini in Arabic.

The Diwan was Egypt's governing council consisting of motley groups of people with conflicting interests, but what united them under one roof was that each needed the other. The official ruler of Egypt was Abu Bakr al-Trabolsi, whom they called Bakir Pasha, the Ottoman governor. Though he was appointed by the Sultan, his real authority was only nominal. The real power was in the hands of the Mamelukes, who were also called "Egyptian princes". Though they were called Egyptians, they were not Egyptians; on the contrary, they despised real Egyptians, did not mix with them, and treated them harshly and brutally. Originally from the Caucasus, two of them, Ibrahim Bey and Murad Bey, were from Georgia. They shared power among themselves, an unusual situation. The usual case was that when the ruler died, the new ruler was the one who can eliminate all his rivals. But this time, after the death of their chief and master Abu al-Dhahab, none of them could destroy the other, so they agreed to share power among themselves.

Another group in the Diwan were the Ulema or imams. They were the real Egyptians and represented the scholars of al-Azhar. The Mamluks ruled by the sword, and everyone feared them, but they could not control everything by the sword alone. They needed the imams to ensure the loyalty of the people and the stability of governance in such a strongly religious society. At the same time, while Imams could influence people, they could not suppress any opposition to them, so they needed the power of the Mamelukes to impose order and maintain their position among the people.

The Ottoman governor did not have the power to control the country but instead depended on the fact that the other two parties needed him. The Mamelukes needed him to legitimise them, as they ruled in the name of The Sultan, the caliph of all Muslims. Similarly, the Imams also needed the Ottoman governor because he was the representative of the caliph of the Muslims. The absolute loyalty of the people was to the caliph, whom the public imagined as the pinnacle of glory and power on the earth's surface. They believed that the caliph was ethical, just and rightful and that he could eliminate the Mamelukes if he received news of their injustice, cruelty, and corruption. Held together by the delicate balance between these three parties, life went on.

Murad Bey began the conversation amongst the Diwan by accusing the Ottoman governor of bringing the Franks to Egypt to eliminate the Mamelukes. The governor objected that it was not right to accuse the caliph of the Muslims of allying with the infidels to invade Muslim lands. Murad Bey felt that no one present agreed with him, and so preferred not to respond. The conversation then revolved around how to address the threat coming from Alexandria. They finally decided that Bakir Pasha would send a letter to inform the Sultan of the French invasion. Murad Bey would lead his Mameluke army to confront the French before they reached Cairo on the west bank of the Nile, while Ibrahim Bey led his army along the east bank of the Nile.

Despite the immense power and wealth of the Mamelukes, they made no effort to understand the world around them. Their only understanding of Europeans came from what was known about them during the Crusades several centuries before, and what they learned from the enslaved Europeans who were kidnapped from their villages on the Mediterranean coast by Algerian pirates under the banner of the Sultan and were sold as slaves to Muslims in North Africa. They looked down on Europeans and did not believe that these pale-faced, heavy-tongued, slow-thinking people could in any way be their equal in courage and the arts of war. Murad Bey said to those present "Let the Franks come, and we will crush them under our horses' hooves."

When it seemed that the meeting was coming to an end, one of the imams spoke in a cautious voice about the need to lift the protection granted to the Egyptian Christians as well as the need to kill all of them as a wise defensive step before the arrival of the Franks. He justified that by saying the

Christians would spy for the Franks and help them and would attack the Muslim army from behind. He didn't want to say it, but he said what he said because he was told to do so by others. He noticed from the faces of those present that no one supported this opinion. The topic ended when Bakir Pasha said that Christians were dhimmis under the protection of the Sultan and none of them could be killed unless he committed a crime worthy of death. In confirmation of this, the Diwan issued a decree ordering the public not to attack the Christians, and the town criers went out to announce it.

Al-Fahameen district, Cairo

A large gathering of toiling workers and destitute people whom Cairenes called al- Ja'idiya, or "rabble," began to arrive from everywhere and gather in al-Fahameen in response to Sheikh Abdul Rahman's call for jihad. They were the poor who worked their livelihood each day. Many were armed, though with pipes, sticks, and knives. Their voices were raised, shouting "victory for Islam and Muslims!" and "death to the infidel Franks!". Their numbers increased as the day wore on, and several al-Azhar religious students preached among them and called on them to march towards the houses of the Christians and eliminate them. Loud shouting and chants spread from every side that shook the corners of the neighbourhood:

'Crusaders are coming to eliminate the religion of Islam and violate the honour of Muslims!'

'The Christians are spying for the Franks, helping them, and preparing to attack the Muslim army from behind. Our Jihad is to eliminate them!'

Kill the Christians, and protect the blood, honour and money of Muslims!

'Fight those who do not believe in God and the Last Day and do not forbid what God and His Messenger have forbidden and do not accept the religion of truth, the truth of Almighty God!'

'There is no religion other than Islam; everyone who takes a faith other than Islam is an infidel!'

'The era of dhimmis is over. There is no place in this country for non-Muslims. If they don't become Muslims, they should be killed!'

'The infidels assaulted the sanctities of the Muslims; Jihad is a must!'

Sheikh Abdul Rahman stood near the mosque waiting for news from the Diwan that they had lifted the protection of

Christians so that he could direct the crowd to their homes. He was surprised by the messenger telling him the contrary, and that a decree had been issued not to attack the Christians. He was disappointed in the Ulema what sat in the Diwan and accused them of treason and weakness, but he had no choice other than to ask the Sheikh of al-Ja'idiya and his aides to do what they could to disperse the crowds and leave the attack for another day.

The church

Many Christian Copts gathered around the church, and some entered the churchyard in confusion, bewilderment, and panic. News came to them that the al-Ja'idiya mob was gathering in preparation for an attack on the Christian quarters. The Copts did not have time to flee, and most men were absent from their homes. There had been debate among them about what to do and who to ask for help. Crying and screaming mixed with wailing:

> 'They will kill us all and burn our houses!'
> 'The looks of hate in their eyes terrify me!'
> 'They won't have mercy on my children!'

'They will not regard an elder, and they will not pity a child!'

The young priest Athanasius came from the church and raised his hands to the crowd in the churchyard, urging them to calm down. Then said, in loud voice, trying to cover up the sounds of crying and wailing:

'"God is our shelter and strength, always ready to help in times of trouble. So we will not be afraid even if the earth is shaken and mountains fall into the ocean depths; even if the seas roar and rage and the hills are shaken by the violence." The Lord Almighty is with us. The God of Jacob is our refuge. Indeed, the Lord is good, and his mercy endures forever. By the prayer of Samaan al-Kharraz and the intercession of the Virgin, the eastern mountain was moved from its place and rose into the sky. God, who is our lord, will never leave us. His eye is on us. He is the one who has preserved us and can protect us and save us from all the evils of the world.'

He continued his sermon and reading of the Gospel, trying to calm the crowd and raise his shaky voice so those gathered outside the church could hear as well.

Not long after, some men came in haste to confirm that the mob of al-Ja'idiya had dispersed and that Sheikh Ismail himself had confirmed this and reassured them. This sheikh had high regard among the people, and the Copts respected him; many were reassured, and some began to disperse, but others remained in the church and continued to sing and pray.

As the noise, shouting, and crying subsided, a group of deacons raised their voices in a harmonious Coptic melody, using the words Isoos Bekhrestoos, meaning Jesus the Messiah in the Coptic language:

"I open my mouth with praise.

To our master Isoos Bekhrestoos

Praise Mary and scream and shout"

And the crowd replied with deacons all enthusiastically with one voice:

"Peace be upon you, mother of Bekhrestoos"

Alexandria

The young general Napoleon Bonaparte stood on the high balcony looking at the sea and hearing the roar of the successive waves that would not stop until the end of time. The glow of the sun's disk dimmed as it disappeared behind the distant horizon. A cool, humid breeze from the sea soothed and refreshed his face after the day's heat. After a long, eventful day, all of Alexandria fell under his command. He had just finished dinner, a tasty meal of fresh, cooked Egyptian food for the first time in weeks. Delicious food with good wine accompanied by his generals who surrounded him with admiration and loyalty gave him feelings of satiety and satisfaction. He moved away from his companions and stared at the vast sea before him, ruminating about the events that brought him to this place in Alexandria, filled with relief that everything seemed in good order.

A new order ruled the world. The ancient empires of the Middle East, India and China have been weakened and corrupted, and Europe had awakened from the dark ages to take the leading place in the world. The world-dominating rivalries had become confined to European countries. Intense enmity between France and England followed the French Revolution. France lost its colonies in North America, the Caribbean and India, but Napoleon led France to the supremacy of Europe, and nothing stood in his way other than England. The English subjected French ships and ports to constant attacks; he hated these arrogant Englishmen and their stupid loyalty to their king; they were the last remaining enemy to be conquered in Europe.

Despite Napoleon's young age, his recent victories in Italy earned him much respect, trust and loyalty from his generals and soldiers. He took orders from the French administration but did not fight for that lazy of lawyers. He fought for something else. France was the pinnacle of civilisation, science, and culture in the world. He would lead France to be the mistress of the world, and he would be the master of France. He will follow in the footsteps of Alexander the Great and head east. He was a man of destiny, and it was the right time to begin his path to glory.

The French directory commissioned him to prepare a plan to invade England, but he persuaded them to pursue a different direction in the war. An invasion of England as a modern-day William the Conqueror was only possible with a powerful Navy. France would first need to strip the English of their strengths. The Ottoman Empire was in a state of decline and mired in corruption, and the new powers of Europe seek to share this sprawling empire, and France must take the lion's share of this legacy. Alexander the Great began his campaign by invading Egypt, and this was what he must do. Egypt would be the place where he fulfilled his dreams. Egypt would be a springboard for this conquest, of the Levant, his expulsion of the Ottomans, and his march towards India to help the rebels against the East India Company. This would sever the connection between England and its largest colony. Restoring the ancient Pharaonic Canal between the Mediterranean and the Red Sea would give France an unparalleled strategic advantage. French ships could sail directly through it to India and all the East while English ships would be forced to sail around Africa. Egypt was the geographical key to the world. Napoleon could do much in Egypt, as a first step on the long road to defeating the English to keep them out of his way to glory.

Everything looked exactly right to him. He successfully avoided a serious confrontation with the English fleet in the Mediterranean. On the way, he stopped at Malta and managed to take control of it quickly and declared it a dependency of the French Republic, and he freed many Muslim prisoners and took them with him to help in Egypt. He could safely reach the shores of Egypt with all his ships and equipment. The port of Alexandria needed to be larger for the number and size of the vessels of the French fleet, but he found a suitable place in Abu Qir Bay, east of Alexandria.

He wasted no time and could safely land his troops ashore at night, away from any interference by the English or Egyptian resistance.

There was some resistance when he entered Alexandria at dawn, but that did not bother him much. He knew that several hundred Circassians and a few old cannons in the citadel of Alexandria would not hold out for long and quickly took control of the city. He was disappointed that he did not find in this city any reminiscent of the greatness of Alexander the Great. He knew that he had no time to waste. He needed to start the campaign quickly and take control of Cairo before the Mameluke princes completed their defensive preparations, before the expected British attack, and before the flooding of the Nile, which may create many obstacles that could slow the advance of his troops.

He left his fleet in Abu Qir Bay under Admiral Brueys d'Aigalliers, who had an honourable record of impressive naval work. He knew that Nelson had preceded him in Alexandria by several days and that Nelson would inevitably return to attack the French fleet. Still, he was confident that Admiral Brueys had plenty of time to put the fleet in a robust defensive posture. He was also confident that the Orient, the greatest ship in the world equipped with 120 high-precision guns, longed for its first battle and would successfully repel any of Nelson's cunning offensive plans.

He invested a lot of time and effort in preparing and printing hundreds of copies of a communiqué translated from French into Arabic by some Muslims he had freed from prison in Malta. The communiqué proclaimed that that he came to support Islam and the Caliph of the Muslims and rid Egypt of the oppression and brutality of the Mamelukes. Did the Mamelukes have anything to do with Islam other than the name? They had used Islam for centuries to enslave and plunder the wealth of Egypt, but he would now use Islam to liberate them. Egyptians would be introduced to freedom, equality and fraternity. Napoleon knew the extent of the hostility that had existed between East and West over the ages, but he was confident that his new approach would change this reality. This was the first confrontation between the enlightened civilisations of Europe and the Middle East-which was mired in darkness. He knew a lot about the Mamelukes and their methods of fighting. They belonged to a distant era and were no equal to him. Nothing in Egypt could stand in the way of achieving his dreams.

While the young general was peacefully sipping the remains of a small glass of port, several Maltese Muslims were rushing their horses to Cairo to deliver Napoleon's communiqué from the French. The aides prepared this communiqué in French and revised it by the commander himself before the Muslims of Malta translated it into Arabic. The communiqué was carefully designed to gain popular support in Egypt. However, these assistants did not realize that the Muslims of Malta were not proficient in Arabic and that their dialect differed from that of the people of Egypt; hence the translation was poor and full of linguistic errors.

Northern Mediterranean

In the northern Mediterranean, on the way to the Anatolian coast, Admiral Nelson was seated in the luxurious dining hall of the officers' section of the Vanguard. He was about to finish dinner, sipping a little port wine from a small glass with his dessert. He was joined at the dinner table by the ship's senior officers. As usual, they talked about the day's events and the tasks for the next day, and they were not without their optimism and humour. He did not doubt their high naval skills, loyalty, and respect for his leadership, but even still he was deeply anxious.

Bonaparte's triumphant return from his campaign in Italy sparked a wave of fear across Britain, started by rumours of a repeat of the Norman invasion and the elimination of the British crown. The danger seemed imminent, and everyone moved quickly to confront Bonaparte before he could invade. The Royal Navy felt the most significant burden, as it was them who could counter any attempt to cross the English Channel.

Intelligencers revealed a large gathering of French military ships in the port of Toulon, but the purpose was unclear. Admiral Nelson was tasked with reinforcing the British fleet in the Mediterranean and later tasked with finding the French fleet and destroying it. This was a challenging task, but he had no choice; there was no alternative but to succeed. He couldn't even think about the possibility of failure. Not only because of his fierce loyalty to the king and country and not only because of his intense hatred for Napoleon, who had no regard for God or king, but also because he knew that he had surpassed more experienced colleagues when he took this task and so if failed It would mean the end of his distinguished service in the Royal Navy. His past heroism, even the loss of his right eye and right arm probably wouldn't be enough to save him.

Nelson faced many difficulties and misfortunes from the outset of this mission. He suffered a severe storm while watching the French fleet near the port of Toulon. His ship Vanguard was so severely damaged that he took refuge behind the island of San Pietro and made the necessary repairs in Sicily, which allowed Napoleon's fleet to slip out of Toulon unseen by his scouts. Nelson had no intelligence regarding the destination of the French. Naploeon's capture of Malta and subsequent departure eastward allowed him to regain the scent. Nelson now had the firm view that the French target must be Egypt, and so he set off in pursuit. Napoleon did not intend to invade England after all but would instead cut the connection between England and its largest colony India, which was another reason why he must succeed in accomplishing the assigned task.

When he arrived in Alexandria, he was disappointed to learned that Napoleon was not there. He sent a small boat to the governor of Alexandria, warning him of the coming French invasion and asking him to buy food and supplies for his ships, but he was surprised by the governor's ill-mannered refusal. He knew that this reckless governor had no effective means of defense if the British went to occupy Alexandria and took what they needed by force. But Nelson did not care about the governor of Alexandria and decided to continue with his mission. To find Napoleon was the only thing in the world that mattered most to him at this point in time.

A copy of the French communiqué translated for the people of Egypt when the campaign arrived

"In the name of Allah, the Merciful, there is no God but Allah; he has no son and no partner in his kingdom; From the side of the French, building based on freedom and equality, The great Sari Askar (meaning the top military commander) Prince of the French armies Bonabarta (meaning Bonaparte, as the Egyptian used to pronounce it) let all the people of Egypt know that for a long time, the Mamelukes who dominate the Egyptian country have expressed humiliation and contempt against the French religion and oppressed its merchants with all kinds of abuse and transgressions so now he attended the hour of their punishment and what delayed us for a long time was this group of Mamelukes brought from the countries of Abaza and Circassia corrupt in the good country, the best, which does not exist elsewhere in the whole globe of the earth, but the Lord of the worlds, who can do everything, has decreed the end of their state. O Egyptians, you have been told that I have not go down in these ways except with the intention of

removing your religion, for that is an outright lie, so do not believe it and tell the slanderers that I did not come to you except to save your rights from the hands of the oppressors, and that I am more than the Mamelukes, I worship God Almighty and respect His Prophet and the great Qur'an, and also tell them that all people are equal with God and that the thing that separates them from each other is the mind and the virtues and the sciences only, and between the Mamelukes and the mind and the virtues are conflicts, so what distinguishes them from others so that they should own Egypt alone and take everything best in it? They took the most beautiful slave girls and best-bred horses and delightful residences for themselves. If the Egyptian land was committed to the ownership of the Mamelukes, let them show us the argument that God wrote it for them. But the Lord of the worlds is gracious, just and merciful, but with his help from now on, no one of the people of Egypt should despair at their chances of entering high positions or gaining high ranks. The scholars, the virtuous and the wise among them will manage and correct things for the benefit of the whole nation. Previously, there were great cities, wide bays, and multiplying stores in Egyptian lands, and all of this would not have been removed if it wasn't for the injustice and greed of the Mamelukes, O sheikhs, judges, imams, chiefs and notables of the country, tell your nation that the French are also loyal Muslims, and to prove this, they went down to Great Rome and destroyed the Pope's chair in it, which always urged Christians to fight Islam. Then they went to the island of Malta and expelled from it those who claimed that God Almighty was asking them to fight the Muslims, yet the French at all times became loyal lovers of the Ottoman Sultan's presence and the enemy of his enemies, God perpetuated his sovereignty, and yet the Mamelukes refrained from obeying the Sultan, not complying with his orders, so they only followed their own greed. Blessed then blessed are the people of Egypt who agree with us without delay so that their conditions will be improved and their ranks will be exalted. Blessed also are those who sit in their dwellings, not inclined to any of the warring parties. If they knew us the most, they would hasten to us with all their hearts. But woe then woe to those who depend on the Mamelukes in to fight us, and they will no longer find a way to salvation, and no trace will remain of them.

Article I, all villages located in a circle three hours close to the places that the French soldiers pass through, so they must send their agents to the Sari Asker, so that the referred may know that they obeyed him and that they erected the French flag, which is white, navy and red.

Article Two: Every village that stands against the French military will be burned with fire.

Article Three: Every village that obeys the French military must also erect the Ottoman Sultan's flag. Long live the one we love.

Article IV The sheikhs in every county must immediately seal all livelihoods, houses and properties that belong to the Mamelukes, and they must be very diligent so that not the slightest thing in them is lost.

Article V The duty of the sheikhs, scholars, judges and imams is that they remain in their jobs, and every one of the people of the counties remains in his home reassured. As well as continuing prayer in the mosques as usual, and the Egyptians as a whole should thank God Almighty for the end of the Mameluke state, shouting God save the French military and the Sultan, God curse the Mamelukes and improve the state of the Egyptian nation.

Witten in the Alexandria camp in 13 of the month Misdoor, in the 6th year of the French Republic's day, meaning in the last Day of the month of Muharram in the year 1213 (Hijri year) ended. I quoted it literally."

Abdul Rahman Bin Hassan al-Jabarti

From the book "Wonders of Antiquities in Biographies and News"

Cairo 1798.

Julien, the artillery officer

He had witnessed many events involving anger, protest, revolution, and war. He had not known peace for years. He had enjoyed a quiet life as a child in a small village on the outskirts of Paris, where his father worked as a manager of a coal mine and his mother as a nurse. He was the eldest of three siblings; he received a good education, completed high school and enrolled at the Sorbonne to study history and literature.

France was mired in debt after the Seven Years' War and the American War of Independence, and the country experienced years of poverty and hunger. It was no secret that Julien's parents were involved in political activities; he noticed frequent meetings and audiences of people in his house, including many of the poor from the villages. When his father lost his job, Julien could not proceed with his studies, so he left Sorbonne and began to think about what to do.

Life changed in May 1789, and the era of enormous events began. One day, his parents asked him to stay at home with his brothers as they went together to Paris with many poor people from the village. They all participated in the storming of the Bastille prison, and his mother later participated in the women's march to Versailles Palace. No one imagined that these events could ever happen. He joined his parents in enthusiastically supporting the revolution and its principles. He was horrified by the Prussian and Austrian invasion of his country to eliminate the revolution. After seeing the French army repel their attack at Valmy, he decided to join the military to defend France and the revolution. Defending France was not his only motivation; he also thought of helping his parents after his father became unable to work; and helping his two younger brothers get into university to achieve what he could not.

He joined the artillery corps, where he heard about the brilliant young officer Napoleon Bonaparte. Bonaparte was also an artillery officer who had served in the Royal French Army and it did not take long before becoming a prominent commander in the Revolution. Julien was trained on one of the modern heavy guns with tremendous destructive power that could be used to demolish castle walls. He loved his work and mastered it. He was ordered to join the young commander Bonaparte's forces as they campaigned in Italy and returned with the army victorious, full of admiration for the heroic commander. He was pleased to learn that he had been chosen, along with many of those who participated in the Italian campaign, to be under the command of General Bonaparte again in a new campaign whose destination was not announced.

He loved France and was proud of everything French. He was very fond of nature and village life and preferred it to life in Paris. He especially enjoyed hiking in the forest with his dog, surrounded by pine and oak trees. He found peace and comfort in the ground that was covered with fern and heather, with bluebells and daffodils flowers scattered everywhere and butterflies hoovering up, complete with goldfinch and blackbird tweets spreading the spirit of beauty. A charm felt by those who knew it well. He liked to remember the meadows and the vast space when the sunrise was seen filling the world with light and when the darkness of the night scattering the stars in the sky. He loved the green Alps and their snow-white crowns, rivers' violent flow and gentle streams' tranquillity. Seeing this splendour and beauty around him gave him the feeling that he was not poor. He felt as if he owned the earth, the sky, the stars, the sea, the river, the waterfall and the birds.

He was also fascinated by the world outside of France and longed for the opportunity to see it; he saw the marvel of nature in Italy but imagined that other worlds might be very different from what he was used to.

His father's cousin was a merchant who lived in Egypt for several decades and returned to live close to him in the village. Julien learned much about Egypt from him. This relative loved Egypt and the Egyptians and had not wanted to return to France. He was only forced to do so in the end because of the Mameluke princes' intransigence, their mistreatment of European merchants, and the imposition of exorbitant customs on their trade. All of these difficulties were bearable, but what really forced him to leave were the repeated raids on his commercial convoys by bandits of Arab Bedouins in the desert and the inability or unwillingness of the Mameluke princes to protect them, perhaps so that the Bedouins would not attack their own caravans. Hence, he had no choice but to leave his happy life in Cairo, which he did with great reluctance.

Julien's cousin told him that the Mameluke princes were originally slaves brought from Eastern Europe and the Caucasus who then took control of Egypt, and they did not treat the native Egyptians better than they treated the

Europeans. Julien heard about the peaceful life his merchant cousin had lived among the Egyptians and the close friendships he had made with many of them. Julien listened with wonder at the stories of life in Cairo's al-Muski neighbourhood, where the Europeans lived, and about how the Egyptians used to call them Franks. The Franks were not the only Christians; there were also the Copts, the native Christians, al-Arwam, the Greek Orthodox and al-Shwam, the Christians from the Levant. It might appear that Christians in the country were humiliated because they were not treated equally. They had to wear small blue or black turbans and were not allowed to wear large ones or luxurious clothes, carry weapons, or even ride mules and horses like Muslims. On the face of it, this might seem to be the case. Still, his relative explained, in reality, these Christians enjoyed power and influence, and were respected by most categories of Egyptians. They did not face any threat except from a few young imams of al-Azhar, who could stir up the commoners and the lower classes against Christians from time to time.

His cousin told him about many things in Cairo that evoked his imagination and excitement. The architecture of mosques, Islamic decorations, the citadel, al-Azhar and the rest of Cairo's neighbourhoods, where the Egyptians who lived in each lane all pursued a particular profession that children inherited from their parents and grandparents. Julien heard about the Egyptians' skills, love of life, their tendency to joke and laugh, and many fascinating market vendors and hawkers that could be found. He also told him about the vast green fields, the endless desert, the immense pyramids of unmatched size and brilliance, and the majestic life that could be lived on the banks of the Nile. He also taught him many Egyptian words and phrases.

Compared to the poverty level in his village, Julien's cousin returned from Egypt with a vast fortune. He was able to buy land and a large house. Julien had hoped that joining the army might enable him to do the same: return to the village and purchase land. Unlike his cousin, he loved France and could not contemplate that he would live anywhere else. No matter how long he stayed abroad, he would return to his village.

He maintained friendships with his schoolmates and university colleagues even after he left the Sorbonne. He was pleased to learn that four of his friends had been selected for the scientific expedition accompanying General Bonaparte's new campaign and he welcomed the opportunity to enjoy their company.

At the agreed time, the tens of thousands of people chosen for the campaign under Commander Bonaparte gathered in the Mediterranean port of Toulon, where a considerable fleet was waiting to carry them across the sea. This small port had never seen such a gathering of this number of ships prepared to take them to the chosen destination that had been kept a secret until now. Before they departed, the young commander gave a speech that did not disclose their goal but excited the troops by promising them adventure, booty, and land when they returned home. He specifically mentioned they would receive five hectares each, reviving Julien's hopes.

Julien met his friends on the same ship, and they talked about the past years and their expectations for the campaign. Commander Bonaparte had previously concealed the real purpose of the planned campaign from the English spies by calling the expedition the "Army of England," and spreading rumours that he was going on vacation to Germany with his wife. Julien's friends, in the scientific expedition, were aware of some details that others did not know because of their proximity to the campaign's leaders. They knew from the large size of the scientific expedition and the sheer amount of scientific equipment and tools they took with them that the English coast might not be the goal of their expedition and that they might study a less civilised place, somewhere in the eastern Mediterranean. They were full of anticipation and excitement about the country where they would dock this enormous fleet. Could it be Egypt? That was what Julien wished for, but there was no way to know. They just had to wait.

The enormous fleet made its way into the Mediterranean Sea towards the east seemingly confirming their suspicion amid many speculations from others. At Corsica, more ships joined the fleet, increasing the size of the force heading to the unknown destination to thirty-six thousand men in addition to many thousands of military engineers, doctors, pharmacists, nurses, scientists, artists and writers in addition to chefs and administrative teams. The total number was more than fifty-four thousand souls. They passed Sicily without stopping disappointing the expectations of some.

It became known to everyone at this time that the English Admiral Nelson commanded a large division of the Royal Navy in search of the French fleet, and this caused an atmosphere of discomfort and concern. The fleet arrived in Malta, and this was an opportunity for the friends to see

Valetta and its large fort. They then continued eastward, and the friends expected at that time their destination could be Egypt. That was the time Bonaparte had chosen to reveal to his army that this was true. He told them: "The genius of liberty, which made you, at her birth, the arbiter of Europe, wants to be a genius of the seas and the furthest nations" and "It will have a massive effect on the world's civilisation, carrying culture back to the land that was the cradle of science and art of all humanity." The friends were overwhelmed by anticipation, suspense, and dreams of what awaited them in Egypt- exploration, research, and discoveries.

For centuries, Europeans knew nothing about Egypt except what was mentioned in the Bible and what Herodotus wrote. What this Greek traveller revealed was enough to arouse fascination and imagination. The few manuscripts written by more recent European travellers, only increased its charm and mystery. These travellers talked about the enormous pyramids, the monumental statues, the meticulously constructed temples of Upper Egypt and the great river that the Egyptians call the Sea of the Nile. Julien's friends knew much about Egypt from what was published and what they heard from Julien, who shared everything he had learned from his merchant cousin. Perhaps Bonaparte himself read a lot about Egypt in his childhood. They were filled with elation and enthusiasm, and they kept talking about it until they reached Alexandria. They arrived late at night, but the commander insisted on going down to the beach without waiting until morning. Julien left his friends to go with his battalion, hoping to meet them again in Cairo.

Zainab, the songstress

Everyone knew she was not like any other songstress, not just because she no longer sang, but also because she was strong-willed, resolute, respectful, and full of pride. Her influence already strong amongst the Egyptians, spread to the Frenchmen as well. She ran one of those new houses of food in al-Azbakeya frequented by French officers and soldiers who called it a "restaurant."

Her upbringing was not like that of other songstresses, as she came from an affluent family from one of the villages of the Sharqiya in the Nile delta, and her father was a wealthy merchant. They lived in a large house in al-Husseiniya. Her mother gave birth to many children, but most died in infancy, and only she and her several years younger brother Ahmed, survived. Zainab remembered her early life as a sweet dream. For years she lived happily in the large house where a maid and three enslaved people helped her mother manage the house. She was used to getting everything she wanted and spent time playing with her peers in the neighbourhood, joined by her little brother. She knew of nothing but fun and play; she knew only smiles and joy. She was a beautiful child, and everyone talked of her charm and sweet voice when she sang with her peers. Her father was her hero, she admired his skill and speed in equestrianism. She remembered his majestic form as he skillfully rode his mare to travel and conduct his affairs, and he often took her with him. On the back of his mare, they roamed around the city enchanted by the views of the Nile and the fields. Her father used to travel for business most of the time, and she treasured her father's company when he was present in Cairo between his travels. In her father's absence, she longingly awaited his return. When she saw his mare in the yard and knew that he had arrived, so she used to run to him and throw herself into his arms as if she did not want to leave him. Her father's returns from his travels were her happiest times, as he used to bring her toys and sweets, and she loved going to the kitchen store room, which they call al-karrar to taste the wide varieties of food that her father brought from faraway lands. Her father's tales of his travels in the desert and to cities in faraway places fascinated her.

It was easy for her to notice that her brother Ahmed was the centre of her father's attention, and her father used to talk a lot about the need to prepare him to be a brilliant merchant so he could take over his affairs. He used to talk much about Ahmed and did not hide his pride and pleasure in his young son in front of others, but that never diminished her great affection for her father because he also gave her a lot of love and tenderness. Her father's intense love for Ahmed also became her own and she also made him the centre of her attention. She cared for him as if she were his second mother. Her father sent Zainab to al-Kotaab, a primitive school that taught students to read Arabic and Qur'an, which was unusual for a girl and did not last long. Still, she wanted to learn more, so her father hired an Areef, a primitive teacher, for private lessons at home, so she learned reading, writing and some arithmetic.

She remembered very well how those happy days ended like a dream. She was playing with her peers in front of the house when she noticed that her brother was sitting on the ground, unable to stand. The maid came and carried him inside, and Zainab saw her mother's alarm as she tried to figure out what had happened. Ahmed was unable to move his legs, and her father came home and hurried over to examine his young son. She remembered well the look of horror in her father's eyes when he realised that little Ahmed had been paralysed.

The days of happiness were gone, and tribulations and afflictions began. For the first time, Zainab experienced what misery was. Life in the big house changed, and many menders, primitive doctors and healers frequented with various medicines and prescriptions to treat Ahmed. It was all to no avail. His father took him to distant places in search of someone who could heal his son, and his mother took him to al-Sayyida and al-Hussain shrines and to all the shrines of the righteous Sheikhs whom she knew or whom she heard about from a friend or neighbour, but nothing changed. The mother decided that Ali, their Nubian slave, would take care of Ahmed all the time and allocated a donkey to help him carry Ahmed on his travels outside the house. Zainab's heart was broken when she noticed the impact of her brother's illness on her mother and father. Smiles and laughter had disappeared and were replaced by anxiety and sadness. This was not the case with Ahmed though. His paralysis appeared as if it hadn't touched his soul, and he remained as satisfied and calm as before. Ali was skilled and loyal in caring for Ahmed and would take him wherever he wanted.

No one paid attention to the many stray dogs in the lane. One of them approached her brother, and a strong friendship began between them, and over time, this dog became a permanent companion to her brother. Her mother noticed the dog became a pleasure to her son, she allowed the dog to enter the house and accompany Ahmed. Hence, the dog became a companion to Ahmed wherever he went, standing from a distance away to wait for him until he finished studying at al-Kotaab or meeting his friends and returning home with him.

The passing of days was no longer the same. Many things changed, and she noticed that her mother was very economical in the house's expenses and that some of the belongings of the big house had disappeared. This did not bother her much, and she was satisfied when she saw Ahmed happy in the company of his dog and Ali's care and attention. One day her father was away on business, as usual, and she and some of her young friends were at a neighbour's house when one of them told Zainab that she saw that her father had just returned from travelling. Zainab hurried back home to warmly cuddle her father as she always did. When she arrived home, she was surprised that her father's mare was not there and that there were several men she had never seen before standing in the courtyard and in front of the door. She hurried to open the door and ran inside. What she saw stunned her. She wondered with horror who was this man who was crying like a woman? He looked like her father; could it really be him? And why was her mother screaming madly at him? Zainab then saw that her mother had turned to her with a look of panic in her eyes as if she did not expect her arrival at that moment. Zainab froze in place and did not say a word. She never wanted to remember the grave events of this day and the subsequent afflictions and hardships that followed.

Years passed before she understood the events of that painful day. She knew that her father had neglected his trade and spent his vast wealth trying to find a cure for Ahmed. He resorted to healers, witch doctors, righteous sheikhs and Christian saints' shrines, magicians, witches, fortune tellers, charlatans and anyone claiming magic powers. Zainab also knew that her mother had tried hard to support him, and she pushed him to pay attention to his work. Her mother strongly objected to spending so much on treatments that did not work. But her father remained firmly attached to the hope of finding a cure for his son and kept seeking anything that gave him a glimmer of hope. The mother strongly warned him that many people claimed healing power to take his money, but he did not listen.

Zainab also knew that her father, like most wealthy people, hid his wealth from the eyes of Mameluke princes and their associates, and her mother found a safe secret place. It was a small underground storeroom in the wall of an abandoned well in the house's backyard. Accessible by three steps, it could only be opened by raising one of these steps. When the mother saw that her father was squandering his wealth, she stopped him from spending their hidden dinars. But she did not know that her father was secretly taking from this hidden wealth, until the dinars were utterly exhausted. He could no longer repay the money he had borrowed, and so on that painful day, the men had come to seize their belongings.

Another series of pains and stresses began. They sold the remaining contents of the house and everything they owned but kept the house itself with the help of relatives and friends. The mother, by good management, was also able to keep the donkey and the Nubian slave Ali to serve her brother. Her brother was also allowed to keep his loyal dog because the mother diligently tried to make Ahmed the least affected by the unfortunate events.

The tribulations and grimness continued; her father had been able to find work with one of his fellow merchants, who assigned him to lead a convoy of Egyptian goods to the Levant in exchange for part of the profit. The road through Sinai was unsafe at this time because of the raids of the Arab Bedouin tribes on the commercial convoys, and perhaps that was why the merchant sent her father instead of leading the convoy himself. While her father found this opportunity to compensate for some of his losses, he was unable to find the right way to avoid the Arabs who raided the caravan in the desert. He could have surrendered, left everything, and returned home safely, but he insisted on resisting the thieves, and they killed him. No one could even find his body.

Losing her father was the most harrowing ordeal she had ever faced. She remembered her previous life, joyful and contented, and felt as if she had been betrayed. She had always believed that her happiness would last forever. How could nobody has warned her about the reality of life and the potential for everything to go wrong? Perhaps then she would have prepared herself to face the horrors that befell her. She was sure that somehow, she would see her father coming home again, and for a long time, she could not believe the truth; her beloved father would never come back.

She remained in endless disarray, confusion, demoralisation, and dark misery. She hated her mother so much for being cruel to her father, but over time Zainab noticed the great difficulties facing her as well. It was not easy for her mother to face life alone, trying to provide for and ensure the safety of her children. Zainab's feelings for her mother changed when she saw her dedication to caring for Ahmed and her determination to provide him with all means of comfort. She began to understand that her mother was always the rock on which the family rested and was the mastermind behind her father's wealth. She had done everything in her power to discourage him from wasting his wealth, but to no avail, as her father's intense love for Ahmed and his desperate search for any glimmer of hope in finding a cure blinded his sight and cost him his wealth and life.

Her beloved father's face frequently came back to her mind; the image appeared to her with a smile when Ahmed was happy and appeared frowning if Ahmed faced any stumbling or difficulty. Over time, her turmoil subsided, and she regained her composure. She was determined to do everything in her power to provide for her brother so that the image of her father's face could appear to her smiling again and again.

Zainab had known Badriya since her early childhood. Badriya frequented the wealthy women of the neighbourhood, who saw her as someone of humble origin who did not respect traditions. Yet Badriya was friendly and funny and provided services everyone needed. Women used to turn to her if they needed perfume, toiletries and ornaments, or if they needed a healer, a herbal prescription, a primitive midwife, a songstress or a dancer for happy occasions, or just needed to buy something scarce in the local market. Badriya often talked about Zainab's breath-taking beauty and sweet voice and suggested to her mother jokingly that she could make Zainab a songstress. The mother had previously laughed at the joke, unaware of what was coming in later life.

Badriya was not the only one talking about Zainab's beauty, Zainab used to hear this from many of those around her, and she was admired by the children of the neighbourhood who frequently met to play in the street or the courtyard of a neighbour's house. Hussein, the son of their neighbour Haj Ibrahim, was her closest friend, whom she saw more often than others because their mothers were also very close friends. Zainab noticed Hussein's admiration for her, and she loved it and shared with him sweet childhood memories of innocent children's competition, collecting the fruits and the delicious berries that had fallen from the trees, sharing Ramadan's sweets, and sharing the fear of goblins, orcs, and other horror stories of the ghoul. They also enjoyed watching the folklore poet playing Rababa, his single string musical instrument, putting the words of traditional tales of Abu Zaid al-Hilali, al-Zeinati Khalifa and al-Zeer Salem to music, and around him, listeners from time to time interrupt him with cheers as he narrates with his sweet melodies. She liked to hear her father talking to his friends and her mother talking to her friends, and though she only understood some of it, and she liked to exchange opinions with Hussein about what she heard. Hussein also shared with her the joy of the Hajj season when they used to follow the singers, panegyrists, and Rababa players when they passed through the streets and squares in Mahmal procession with her heart full of spiritual joy when singing with the panegyrist:

"Guide, take me to the prophet to see him with my own eyes

Here is the prophet has travelled and passed over Mina and Mount Arafat"

The days of childhood passed like a dream, then came the tragic events, and the passing of days never returned to how the days had passed before. Zainab noticed a distance and emptiness between her mother and her friend Hussein's mother that she could not understand. She no longer saw Hussein or his mother in her house, and her mother's visits to Hussein's mother stopped, so she no longer saw Hussein, but she remained willing to see him and talk to him whenever she had the opportunity. She noticed that her mother was often absent from the house, and Badriya kept coming to their home more often.

As the years passed, Zainab became a young woman and learned more about life's realities and what was happening around her. She was no longer allowed to mix with boys and stayed home most of the time. Her shape changed, and her body curves increased and became even more beautiful and attractive, and her mind was overwhelmed by the emotions of adolescence. She felt attracted to the boys she was forbidden from seeing and found that she was thinking a lot about Hussein. She used to see him from behind their screened balcony al-Mashrabiya, and noticed his growth in stature, strength and handsomeness, and he became bearded, making him even more handsome. She longed to find a way to see him and talk to him.

Mansour, the merchant

He was a wealthy merchant with significant influence, close to many Mameluke princes and the ulema of al-Azhar. He frequently spent the evening with other wealthy friends in the grand house of Haj Mustafa in al-Sanadikya. Some of them needed favours from him, that required him using his influence with the princes. He was known as an insider who knew what was happening behind closed doors. He was also seen as a bighearted man who would always help others. Haj Mustafa and his friends had known him for many years. He knew a lot about each of them, but they didn't know much about him and his hidden secrets. If they knew the truth about him, they wouldn't keep him as a friend. They lived their lives in ease and comfort while he lived through so many horrific events and horrors, and endured so much pain that he was left determined to not take on any more. Life had taught him how to protect himself and to get what he wanted.

His painful old memories never left him, and there seemed to be nothing he could do to get rid of them. They were always there in his mind to haunt him and deny him peace and serenity.

His childhood began as it did for many of Cairo's children. He was one of seven siblings living with their parents in a small townhouse. His father was a butcher; he was less well-off than some, but what he earned from his small shop was enough to satisfy the modest needs of the family. Mansour loved his father very much. He was the eldest of his siblings and was sent to help his father in the shop. He admired his father's skill in cutting and arranging meat, and his father began to teach him some basic skills, but he did not find dealing with the carcass and using a knife and cleaver an easy job. As he struggled his father would smile and guide him on the best way to cut different parts of the animal carcass. His father was also friendly with customers who were always kind to Mansour talking nicely to him while he stood trying to help his father. The days passed like they passed every day in the neighbourhood, and his family was happy and content. Mansour enjoyed working with his father and playing with his siblings; there was nothing to disturb his peace of Mind.

Then came this dreadful and unforgettable day. He was not with his father that morning of this fateful day but had returned to catch up with him in the afternoon. He was surprised by the immense crowd standing around his father's shop. With difficulty, he squeezed his head through the masses and pushed grown-ups aside to see al-Muhtasib, the chief of trade and supply police, with his men. They beat and cursed his father while the crowd watched. He later learned that someone had reported his father to al-Muhtasib for cheating customers in weighing the meat giving them less than what they paid for. Without raising any questions, he came with his men. After delivering a severe beating and humiliating of his father in front of the neighbours, they put a large ring through his father's nose and hung a large piece of meat on his neck adorned with bells and jingles. They put his father backwards on a donkey and paraded him through the neighborhood. Mansour cried, screamed, shouted, and rushed trying to reach his father, but al-Muhtasib's men pushed him away and threw him to the ground. The procession, a traditional one to humiliate a cheat known as al-Tagrees was led by a man who rang a bell and went around the neighbourhood. Mansour hurried after the procession screaming, crying and begging the men of al-Muhtasib to release his father, but he did not get anything in return other than insults and kicks. He watched with horror as the pedestrians mocked his father and ignored his pleas and screams. Several hours later, the procession returned to where it started. al-Muhtasib's men dragged his father to their house and hung him on the door, leaving him there and preventing anyone from helping him. Mansour saw his father's face grimacing in pain and unable to speak. Mansour continued to scream and shout, begging everyone he saw to help his father. Finally, near sunset, the men of al-Muhtasib threw his father on the ground and went on their way.

Some neighbours rushed to carry his father inside and left him on his bed, unable to move. He noticed that the expression of pain on his father's face had changed to pallor and reproach, and his eyes seemed to be blurred as if he could not see Mansour or anything in the room. His mother and siblings were crying and trying to comfort his father and offer him food and drink. Mansour was horrified when he noticed that his father seemed to feel nothing and didn't realise what was happening around him. Everyone went to sleep, and he was crammed into bed amid his siblings, continuing to cry, until he fell asleep.

Suddenly, before dawn, he awoke to the sound of his mother screaming and crying out in panic as loud as she could:

'Help me, help me, people help me.'

He quickly got up. The rigid, frozen gaze in his father's eyes and the pallor of his face struck him. These were enough to show him for the first-time what death was. The neighbours came quickly; and the house was crowded with many men and women. Shouting rose from every direction, as well as ululating, wailing, and screaming. His heart broke to see his mother slapping her own cheeks very hard and throwing dust on her head while screaming.

The events of this dismal day were only the beginning of a long series of hardships and tribulations for Mansour. Everything had changed. Their house and shop were taken from the family to pay off his father's loans, and they ended up living in a small room that could barely accommodate a mother and seven children. Dinner changed from creamy meat with potatoes, pumpkins or taro to just bread dipped in a pinch of salt or sprouted beans soup, and the bedding changed to burlap roughness and sleeping on the floor. With the help of some relatives, his mother began to earn a modest income by selling sweets. His mother had to wake up before dawn prayers to start preparing the sweets, while his siblings were in the market buying ingredients. Once the sweets were made, his siblings would take them to sell in different markets until the day was over.

As for Mansour, he settled down to work as a butcher shop boy in a street nearby, but this butcher was not kind to him like his father was; Mansour did not yet have enough skill, and the employer was harsh with him, insulting and beating him for any delay or mistake. He no longer met his boyhood friends because they worked with their parents most of the day, and Mansour hated working in the butcher's shop. He began to be absent and spend the day aimlessly roaming the streets and the neighbourhood lanes. He got to know many of the young people who also had a harsh life and were aimlessly wandering the streets like him.

One day he found someone who told him that he could earn money without working at a butcher's shop; there was an easier way. He introduced Mansour to Mu'allim Bashir.

Bashir did not manage a workshop as the rest of the men with the title Mu'allim did, instead, he taught children to steal for him. Each day, he sent them to different places in Cairo and at the end of the day took what they had stolen and gave some money, depending upon how much each could steal. Mansour discovered that theft was much easier and more profitable than butchering. He quickly learned to steal from homes, shops and cafés wherever the opportunity arose. It did not matter what he stole because Mu'allim Bashir welcomed everything and gave him money at the end of the day. His mother did not know how Mansour spent his days because she was so busy preparing and selling sweets and had no time left to think about it. She was exhausted at the end of the day, sleeping deeply before starting her new day before dawn. She was simply content that Mansour brought her a few half dinars from time to time, and thought no more of it.

Life was not easy for Mansour, as he was caught stealing several times. Because of his young age, the owners of the stolen goods were satisfied with just beating him after recovering what was stolen. He was kicked and punched many times with no harm done, but what he feared most was this firm slap on the face, not only because of the severe pain it caused but because of the dizziness and nausea that haunted him the rest of the day and the bruises that remained on his face for several days after the slap.

He then realised that there was much worse than kicks and slaps. One hot summer day, he saw an opportunity to steal some figs, which he loved so much. It seemed to him that the shop owner had left the shop on an errand, so he hurried and quickly took as many figs as he could hold in two hands. As he started to run away, he felt a heavy hand holding the neck of his robes from behind and choking him. He expected that the slaps and kicks would follow, so he started crying and pleading, thinking that maybe his pleas would reduce the severity of the beating, but none of that happened. The huge man who owned the shop dragged him violently to a place in the back hidden behind a stack of large empty fruit baskets and threw him over a chair. Quickly, before Mansour figured out what was happening to him, he felt the weight of this enormous man's body almost stopping his breath, the man's strong fingers lifting his robes, and the man's stinking smell suffocating him. A few moments passed before he felt a tremendous pain that he had never felt before in his short life. Several minutes passed before it became clear to him that he had been raped. Mansour had known that the same had happened to many of his peers, and the boys used to warn each other about certain men who targeted them for this shameful act. And now he realised that what had happened to others had also happened to him. Afterwards, he was left lying alone behind the shop while the miscreant culprit talked to his customers as if nothing had happened.

Some advice from his peers helped him endure the pain for several days, but he felt outraged and disgusted. He hated himself deeply, and wished for death; he knew what loss of honour and dignity meant. He was horrified that many of his peers did not give much importance to the matter because it was not uncommon, but that did not make him feel any better about what happened to him. He felt alone, facing a cruel hard life.

He was not physically that strong, but as time went by, he gained a leadership position among his peers. He became close to Mu'allim Bashir because of his intelligence and ability to read the minds and hearts of others and understand what was going on around him. Such skill helped him get to know and get close to many influential people in the neighbourhood. He found that reporting what others were up to and what they saying about these influential people with a dose of flattery and deception was an easy way to get closer to those in power in the neighbourhood. Years passed, and over time his status increased to the point that he did not need to steal or work for Mu'allim Bashir.

He understood the people's suffering caused by the exorbitant taxes imposed on them by the Mameluke princes. He knew that the princes used the Copts to collect and calculate taxes, and it was not difficult for him to realise that the people hid their wealth so that the princes would not seize it. No one could keep their wealth unless they were close to the princes or the ulemas. At first, he gained the trust of the Coptic Mu'allim in charge of collecting taxes in the neighbourhood by informing on some of those hiding their wealth. The Coptic Mu'allim was careful not to miss any of this hidden wealth because this would expose him to the full brutality of the princes. Hence, he fully appreciated the importance of informers like Mansour. He gained a lot from his closeness to the Coptic Mu'allim before he realised that the real power was with the Mameluke princes and that the best way to protect himself from harm and evils of life was to get closer to them. They were the ones who had the swords and soldiers. He knew the princes needed to understand what was happening around them, who was conspiring against whom, and who was not loyal to them. His influence increased, and as he became closer to those in power, his sources of information multiplied and diversified. His ability to know what was happening behind closed doors increased the prices paid to him for his information about the secrets of others.

At the time, the control of the country was divided between two men ,Ibrahim Bey and Murad Bey. Ibrahim Bey was the official sheikh of the country, which literally meant the civil governor of Cairo but was, in effect, the ruler of all Egypt. Murad Bey, however, was just as powerful and was his rival in all matters of power. Mansour even knew what was going on in the princes' palaces and realised that it was not wise to try to get close to both simultaneously. He would have to decide to dedicate his loyalty to one or the other. Through his skill in understanding the forces that shaped events, he knew that Murad Bey was the mightier and more cunning of the two and was so determined to reach him, gain his trust, and pledge his loyalty. He put much effort and money into getting close to Murad Bey's inner circle until he finally gained access to him with some information about Ibrahim Bey's followers that was difficult for anyone else to know.

Murad Bey trusted no man and regarded all people as his enemies, even his closest followers, and violently and brutally acted against those whose loyalty he doubted. Still, he was also generous and hospitable to those he thought were of interest to him. Mansour knew the danger of getting close to Murad Bey. He knew that he could be subjected to his brutal revenge if Murad Bey had the slightest doubt of his loyalty or felt that he did not need him anymore. Still, Mansour succeeded where others did not, and became one of the few to whom Murad Bey listened attentively and one of the few to receive his generous gifts. He didn't need Murad Bey's money as much as he needed his influence to outperform all those who competed with him in his trade. His proximity to Murad Bey allowed him to obtain commercial deals without customs or access to goods that his competitors could not reach, and with the money he received, he bought the loyalty of more collaborators everywhere who could convey to him everything that was happening around them, so he had knowledge of what was going on behind closed doors in the palaces of princes, the corridors of al-Azhar, the homes of the notables, and even amongst al-Ja'idiya, in their rustic neighbourhoods.

People were moaning, complaining, and speaking out about the injustice done to them, but that didn't bother Murad Bey because none of those people had a sword. What really mattered to him was what the other princes were up to, particularly those close to or working for Ibrahim Bey. The two men always conspired against each other, and many wanted to eliminate him. Murad Bey was also keen to know what was happening between the imams of al-Azhar because he knew their considerable influence on the people and always wanted to ensure they were under his control. He was particularly keen to learn about some of the young al-Azhar imams and students who could incite hate and violence against Christians and Jews and provoke al-Ja'idiya to attack them. Murad Bey did not mind this type of violence because it diverted the attention of the commoners away from the idea of mounting a revolution against him. Still, he was keen to keep this violence under his control because he relied on Christians to manage all the state's accounts and administration. Murad Bey trusted only them because a Christian, whether rich or poor or a priest, thought only of keeping themselves safe from harm and never dreamt of competing for power.

Mansour knew how to be close to Murad Bey and how to be trusted by him and knew how to make Murad Bey feel always in need of his services, not only by providing him with what he needed to know about what was happening around him behind closed doors but also by spreading fake news and information. Murad Bey used misinformation to help him restrain Ibrahim Bey and extend his own influence and control over Egypt.

Mansour made a vast fortune from trade and became known as influential, generous, and willing to help his friends and those in need. His circle of friends included imams of al-Azhar, the wealthy class of Muslims, and Coptics and other Christians in Egypt, including the European merchants in the al Muski neighbourhood. Over the years, he had no qualms about living a double life. On the one hand, he was the wealthy merchant whom everyone respected and appreciated, and on the other hand, he was the eye of the military; he was the spy who secretly supplied Murad Bey with information on everything that went on between the various sects of people in Cairo, and who spread whatever lies Murad Bey wanted to spread among the Cairenes. Mansour felt that he had overcome all his childhood fears and would remain safe and unhurt as long as Murad Bey supported him.

Hussein, the blacksmith

Hussein lived in the shadow of his father who gave him the name of the grandson of the prophet Mohamed. People knew him more as the son of Haj Ibrahim than by his own name. He lived a luxurious and carefree life in a large house in al-Husseiniya. His mother was keen to keep him satisfied and comfortable, assisted by servants and slaves. In his childhood, he spent his time playing with children in the courtyard or front of the house, but the one of the children who attracted him most was Zainab. She was the beautiful child everyone loved to play and talk with. She was always laughing, skilled in playing hopscotch, and nicely jumping on one foot. He knew her better than others because her house was nearby and her mother was a friend of his mother. They often exchanged visits, and Zainab was always with her mother. Hussein's mother noticed that her son was keen on Zainab's company, and she used to smile happily at that and sometimes rewarded him by bringing Zainab to play with him. Zainab went with him to al-Kotaab, and she was the only girl among the boys. He noticed her intelligence, but she was not allowed to continue. As time went by, she was prevented from attending at all and later she was not allowed to mix with boys of the neighbourhood, but Hussein was keen to find the opportunity to talk to her when their mothers were visiting each other. His mother loved Zainab and prayed that her son's destiny would be to marry her. The days passed, and they reached the age at which girls should be separated from boys, so it was no longer easy for him to see Zainab. He was still keen to talk to her whenever he had the opportunity to do so, even if it was behind his mother's back. He knew nothing of Zainab other than as a beautiful child who always smiled when she spoke to him. He found pleasure in talking to her about whatever came to mind. The conversation touched on competition in play with their peers and then spoke about the events of their day at home, about their parents, and the exciting stories they used to hear from grown-ups when they visited each other. They also talked about serious things, like heaven and hell on the day of judgement, the mosque, the shrines, the miracles that happen in the name of the virtuous sheikhs, and their participation in their parents' prayers.

He reached the age when he should start working, and his father was preparing him to be his right-hand man in running his vast businesses. His wealthy father owned several blacksmith workshops and held real estate, farmlands, and a thriving trading business. After learning to read and memorise the Qur'an in al-Kotaab, his father sent him to one of his blacksmith workshops to learn blacksmithing which he loved. He became skilled in it but did not have enough time to continue, as he had to accompany his father to also learn about agriculture and trade. Hussein learned loyalty to Islam in his early childhood. His father used strictly observe the need to pray the day's five prayers, and he also repeated supplications to God and cited verses from the Qur'an and the Hadith in all his conversations with others. His father was keen to take him and his brothers to the mosque to pray. He found satisfaction and peace in reading and reciting verses from the Qur'an and in the fact that everything that happened in the world was governed scrupulously by the justice of God. His father was a Sufi who used to hold dhikrs and take Hussein to dhikr circles. Hussein liked them because the rhythmic chants of the Sufis took him to a venerable, heavenly realm. He loved the songs of the dhikr circles and enthusiastically chanted with his father with the singers:

"Help, relief, O' our master Hussain, help O' father of Zayn al-Abidin.

Help, relief, O' our master Hussain, the son of the daughter of the messenger of Allah"

His deep religious feelings did not prevent him from longing to see Zainab and talk to her whenever possible. Days passed, and meeting Zainab became problematic, as their parents no longer allowed it, and sometimes he had to wait a long time to find the opportunity to talk to her.

He reached the age when his body changed, so he became tall, strong, and handsome and grew a beard like his father. The sexual feelings of adolescence aroused him, and all his dreams and fantasies were all centred around Zainab. The children of wealthy people like him could satisfy their sexual needs with the slave girls, but Zainab was always who he longed for. The veil on her face did not hide her domineering beauty, her loose dress failed to hide how svelte and graceful her tall body was, and his mind often drifted to imagining the charming beauty underneath. It was not easy for him to hide his feelings from his mother, who noticed his interest in any news about Zainab. She reassured him that she would betroth her to him when the time was right.

The world changed, and that "right time" he was waiting eagerly for had never come. Hussein heard the sad news and the misfortune that befell Zainab's family. In the beginning, was the mysterious paralysis that afflicted her brother, then her father's loss of his fortune, and talk about the imminent sale of their house and the possibility of the family leaving the neighbourhood. Finally, there was the death of her father in the desert on the way to Suez. Until then, his mother was sympathetic to Zainab and her mother and tried to help them, but this did not last long. Hussein noted with great sorrow that his mother had completely changed her views about them. Zainab's mother had become an evil she should avoid, and estrangement and disaffection between the two families replaced cordiality and friendship. Hussein could not understand any reason for the change other than that Zainab's mother refused to sell her house and take her children to her husband's relatives in the Eastern Province. Contrary to custom, she decided to work and earn what she could to care for her paralysed son. Zainab's mother had to work with Badriya and was absent from her home for extended periods. She involved Zainab in this work, which Hussein's mother and all the other neighbours strongly condemned and that ended up with complete estrangement and hostility toward Zainab and her mother. Although Badriya was known to everyone in the neighbourhood and frequented their homes, they viewed her as a menial person to be tolerated. They received her in their homes only because of her skills and the many services she performed for them, but it was unforgivable for Zainab's mother to work with her and, worse, involve Zainab in this work. Hussein's dreams collapsed, and his hope that he would become engaged to Zainab and then marry her one day seemed almost impossible.

It happened on 23rd July 1798

French Camp, Giza

Julien sat with several French soldiers resting for a while. At last, they had found enough food, water, and a shady place to rest, and they chatted, filled with satisfaction with what had been achieved and what they had gained from the defeated Mameluke princes. Cairo, their final prize, was within their grasp, with nothing to do other than cross the Nile to be there. No one could now stand in their way to seize Cairo.

Julien reflected on the horrors he had faced on the way between Alexandria and this pleasant place. In Alexandria, he and his friends wandered around the city and were disappointed that he had not found any trace of the ancient grandeur he had heard of. He left his friends and joined his unit when he received orders to march towards Cairo without delay. The army was divided into two parts. The first was directed to marsh towards Rashid to take the Nile Road to the south, which was the route the Egyptians used to take when travelling from Alexandria to Cairo. The second part, which included Julien's unit was to take a shortcut across the desert from Alexandria to Damanhur and from there to Rahmaniya. It was there that the two parts would join together again.

He did not know at the time the dread and detestation that awaited him when crossing the desert. It was boiling, the sun was scorching, there was nothing to shade or protect them from the burning sun, and they didn't have enough water. His throat dried up until it became sore, the heat of the sand burned his feet, the hot air scorched his lungs, and the heavy military uniform became a massive burden in the seemingly endless desert. They found a few wells on the way, but they were quickly emptied of water by thousands of desperate, thirsty soldiers, and then came this mirage that made things worse as it looked like water in the desert when it was actually just more hot air and scorching sun. The road from Alexandria to Damanhour took five days, during which he tasted the scourge of hell. The morale of some of the soldiers broke raising objections and rebellion. His colleagues were falling dead from fatigue and thirst, and the bandits of Arab Bedouin were lurking around, kidnapping or killing anyone who fell behind.

The soldiers forgot military discipline when they reached Rahmaniya and the river Nile could be seen in the distance. They hurried towards the water, and in desperation, Julien could not resist the urge to throw himself in full military uniform into the river and drink the fresh cold water of the Nile to extinguish the scorching sun. He watched with great horror as a colleague who had preceded him into the water by several steps was taken by a massive crocodile which pulled him deep into the river.

The army was not allowed to stay long and continued in a southerly direction towards Cairo. In the Nile Delta, he noticed the stretching green fields and palm trees, and walking became less troublesome, but he noted with disappointment the manifestations of poverty and misery in the small villages scattered in the delta of the Nile and wondered where was the magic of Egypt he had heard so much about?

At Rahmaniya, their comrades who had taken the Rosetta way arrived as planned and continued marching south with them on the west bank of the Nile, followed by a small fleet of guns and supply boats in the river. At a village called Shoubrakheet, the first signs of the enemy appeared. For the first time in several centuries, a European army faced the soldiers of the East. He couldn't believe what he saw; the Mameluke knights and their horses appeared very luxurious and grandiose with bright loose coloured clothes and large turbans studded with precious stones, advancing with their great horses and performing a show of their cavalry skills by swinging their swords in the air, it looked to him more like a festival or a theatrical performance than a battlefield. One of these knights came forward screaming from afar and waving his sword as if to say who dares to challenge me? Julien felt sorry for this idiot who made this mediaeval challenge to their modern warfare; the French met the challenge with a bullet that instantly killed him. The Mameluke cavalry rushed bravely forward in a swift and lightning attack in groups in the manner of the past ages. When they approached the prepared ranks of the French infantry, they received a barrage of bullets stronger than their courage, yet they kept repeating their desperate attempts in vain. It was a brief battle, after which the cavalry retreated and fled to the south, and the French advance continued.

When the French army reached the outskirts of a small village called Imbaba, they saw the fortifications of the Mameluke army waiting for them. They also saw the great pyramids towering in the distance. Bonaparte addressed them, saying, "Soldiers, from the height of these pyramids, forty centuries look down on you."

The French generals had learned the Mameluke method of war from the Battle of Shoubrakheet. Still, the Egyptian Mamelukes did not seem to have learned anything, so they repeated their failed attacks, rushing large numbers of knights forward in a quick surprise attack, with their swords raised in the air. The French held their nerve and waited until the mamelukes were close to their rows stacked in squares then showered them with a hail of bullets they had no way to avoid. The Mameluke knights repeated the futile attacks again and again in a desperate attempt to break through the squares of the French but it was to no avail. Julien noticed that the Mamelukes were fighting valiantly and bravely but with a style of warfare whose reign had long been over. He remembered well one of these knights, who looked like a majestic grand old man in very luxurious, grandiose and pompous clothes, rushing without fear toward the ranks of the French to be shot like his peers. Still, the man continued forward despite his injuries and succeeded in breaking through the first row of the French Square to be met with more bullets. He continued his desperate suicidal attempt until he fell dead. It was clear that skill and recklessly brave chivalry could not be a match for the skill of the French in modern warfare, and it was not an hour before the battle was decided. A few mamelukes managed to flee south and escape with their lives, but the majority who fled westward were trapped between the French and the Nile and had no option but to throw themselves into the river, indifferent to the Nile crocodiles. It was a decisive battle. The losses of the French did not exceed three hundred dead. Still, the fatalities of the Mameluke princes were heavy, with more than six thousand dead. The fields of Imbaba were filled with thousands of Mameluke corpses, and the French soldiers were surprised when they discovered that the dead knights were hiding their gold dinars and precious jewels in their clothes and between the folds of their turbans, a huge fortune was found in each corpse. A long and arduous journey to Imbaba had ended with a quick victory and abundant spoils.

Here, Julien was now sitting resting in the shade, enjoying a cool breeze that refreshed his face after the heat of the day, surrounded by the green fields, palm trees and sparrows chirping on the trees. He also heard the singing of goldfinch and was pleased that this bird existed in Egypt as it reminded him of his village and his homeland France. The rumbling and humming of the French soldiers grew louder when they heard and saw massive fires and explosions on the east bank of the Nile, until they realized this was just the fleeing Mameluke knights burning their boats and detonating their munitions so that the French would not seize them.

Crossing the river and entering Cairo felt like a picnic; no one stood in their way. Cairo seemed to be a large city with many ornate high buildings, and Julien did not find in it the same manifestations of misery and poverty that he had found in the villages of the Delta. He had the opportunity to see one of the palaces of the fleeing princes, which Bonaparte had taken as his residence and headquarters. He was told that it was the palace of al-Alfi Bey, one of the senior Mamelukes, who never had a chance to live in it despite spending a considerable fortune preparing and refurbishing it because he fled with the other fugitives after the battle of Imbaba. The palace that overlooked the river Nile was extreme in its pomp, beauty, luxury and grandeur, with vast gardens he didn't see the end of it full of willow, ornamental plants, palm trees and lots of ripe vineyards whose grapes he found so delicious.

Julien sat with some soldiers in the middle of the greenery, enjoying the ripe fresh grapes they had picked from the many vineyards in the garden and talking:

> 'I have never seen the magnificence, luxury, and greatness of this palace anywhere before.'
>
> 'This starkly contrasts the poor and miserable homes of Egyptians that we saw in the villages of the Nile Delta.'
>
> 'It seems like two states in one country, a state for the Mamelukes and a state for the Egyptians.'
>
> 'This is not much different from pre-revolution France. The world of aristocrats was utterly different from the world of the commoners.
>
> 'Has anything changed?'
>
> 'I look forward to walking around the streets of Cairo and seeing the markets, buildings and mosques.'
>
> 'There are scholars in al-Azhar Mosque who are regarded as highly as those in the Sorbonne; there is a lot in this country to be discovered.'

'Our Citizen General Bonaparte called on everyone to treat the Egyptians gently and to respect their religious beliefs as we did with the Jews and Catholics in Italy.'

Boulaq district, Cairo

The tranquillity, elation, and comfort felt in the camp of the French army at Giza on the west bank of the Nile was in sharp contrast to the bewilderment, confusion, sadness, and dread across the Nile on the east bank at Boulaq. Hussein stood there surrounded by a group of young men behind the barricades they had set up, thinking quickly about what to do. The situation changed every minute with their sense of confusion, chaos, and terror only increasing.

When news about the Franks taking Alexandria first reached Cairo, no one expected events would become so disastrous. At first, everyone was happy and reassured of the power of the Mameluke princes and their ability to deter any invasion. The princes started preparing their defences and fortifications; Hussein was forced to work overtime in the blacksmith workshop to supply what the princes demanded; they took everything they needed from his father's workshops without paying. They were taking what they needed from people by force, and the Egyptians accepted this on the basis that the princes were the ones who defended the homes of Muslims from the infidels who wanted to eliminate the religion of Islam. People noticed that the Mameluke princes were moving their belongings and wealth from their large palaces to safe houses on the outskirts of Cairo and beyond. This frightened them, and some of the wealthy and privileged people thought of fleeing Cairo, but the princes prevented them from going.

Then came the news of the first confrontation between the French and Murad Bey's men in Shoubrakheet. It was a limited confrontation between the vanguards of the two armies and ended in the defeat of the princes. Murad Bey retreated to organise his forces and strengthen his fortifications around Cairo. News of the first defeat alarmed the Egyptians; some began to panic and flee the city, but until now, most Cairenes decided to stay and help the princes repel the invasion. Hussein left his family in al-Husseiniya and hurried with numerous youth companions to Boulaq. He began to prepare the defences, acquiring any weapons they could get, such as pipes, sticks, knives, muskets, and gunpowder. Shops and markets were closed, and everyone went to Boulaq to help set up barricades. Groups of people from Moroccans and Syrian residents were equipped with weapons to assist in its defence. The ulema and imams headed by Omar Makram, the head of the nobles, went out to call for Jihad, exciting the spirited enthusiasm of the masses who flooded the streets chanting and shouting "oh God, oh kind God, God is great, all men of God defend the land and honour of the Muslims, kill the infidels." Everyone became ready and eager to confront the invaders.

Then came the news of disaster in Imbaba; the Mamelukes were defeated, and had fled the battlefield, to return to their luxurious palaces to flee with their harem and the rest of their precious belongings. Ibrahim Bey fled east to the Nile Delta region, and Murad Bey fled south to Upper Egypt. Suddenly the Egyptians realised they had no army to protect them. For many centuries, the Egyptians had only had the Mameluke Princes to defend the land of Egypt; now, the princes had fled, and there was no one to protect the country, and they would become prey to the enemies. At sunset, everyone saw the flames rising high in the sky and the sounds of explosions coming from the bank of the Nile; then news spread everywhere that the Franks were coming. People said that they were killing and burning everything in their path, and they were capturing women to be their slaves. Panic spread, and a night of horror and heinousness Cairo had never seen before began.

Hussein and his companions hurried back from Boulaq to their homes, rushing to help their families escape. People hurried from the city, and panic prevailed as they anticipated enslavement, destruction, and death. Voices rose in supplication to God, women cried and wailed, and everyone tried to find a way to save themselves and their families. Hussein and his family managed to flee to the east, helped by their horses, mules, and donkeys, and saw that many notables and sheikhs did the same. The less fortunate fled on foot, and many women walked with their faces unveiled, carrying their children, praying to God, and crying in the darkness of the night. Some managed to take what they could have with them. Cairo was without an army to protect it and without a ruler to govern it. Chaos, looting and theft prevailed, and the Arab Bedouins attacked the surrounding villages and robbed the fugitives fleeing the city. They took whatever they carried of money and belongings, even stealing their clothes leaving some with nothing to cover their nakedness.

The church

Father Athanasius stayed alone in the church, praying and reading and reciting verses from the Bible and the Agbiya, the prayer book of the Coptic church. He heard the sounds of crying, wailing and shouting outside. Still, he did not run away with others staying to face his destiny. The vizier and sheikh of the country had previously sent Salim Agha, the head of the Janissaries, to the Christians to reassure them of the safety of their lives and properties. They launched the town criers to call for the protection of the Christian subjects and forbid attacking them, but that was not the case. At the beginning of the events, when the Mameluke princes went out to meet the Franks, and chaos spread all over Cairo, al-Ja'idiya mob attacked the houses of the Christians and looted and killed many of them. However, many Christians had left Cairo beforehand in anticipation of events and did not witness the day's chaos after the princes fled. Father Athanasius' loneliness was interrupted by the arrival of a few men with their families and meagre belongings. They could not find a way to escape Cairo and so decided to stay and take refuge in the church and submit to God's will. They kissed the hand of the priest holding the cross and sat around him, listening to his prayers and praying to God with him, asking for help, protection and intercession from the Virgin and St. George.

Old Cairo district, Cairo

In a few hours, the sun would appear, announcing a new day. Broken-hearted Zainab stood looking tearfully at her mother's pale and motionless face, marked by the tranquillity of death. She now had to face life alone. She must be as strong as her mother had been and face the odds with as much courage as her mother did. She had no other choice. Her mother, the strong tigress who knew how to protect her children and the rock everyone leaned on, was now lifeless, and her brother Ahmed was next to her, weeping in silence. He never complained. Zainab was overwhelmed with grief when she remembered what this mother did for her and Ahmed and remembered her strength when faced with calamitous adversities.

After the death of her father, her mother's cousins and her husband's family did not help her much; Zainab's mother did not find anyone to rely on other than Badriya, and the bonds of friendship increased between them; Badriya helped her mother to contact the merchants with whom her late husband had previously dealt with buying goods and then helped her find customers for these goods in different places in Cairo where they were most in need. She did hard work alone for many years. When she was old enough, Zainab helped her, so she knew how hard her mother worked to support them. Badriya found Zainab a job singing at women's gatherings for various occasions. Zainab loved this work, and in a short period, she became very much in demand for her melodious sweet voice that delighted her audiences, and the dinars started flowing fast. She was hoping very much that she would be able to relieve her mother from all the hard work and let her enjoy some life for herself after all these challenging years, but fate did not give her time to achieve this. Now her beloved mother was lying dead. The sun would soon rise with a new day, and the universe would wake up, and then the days would pass as they always passed.

Her mind recalled the horror she had seen that day and what horror that was. The day began with foreshadowing of the coming danger when her mother woke her up in the darkness before dawn, asking for help; Zainab awoke to find Badriya and her mother trying to move a hefty large burlap sack whose contents she did not know. Badriya told them that the Mameluke princes were hiding their wealth in safe houses far from their palaces in anticipation of the next war. Some of them had moved their harems and families outside Cairo as well, and many notables had done the same. She told them that this sack had been sent to her by one of the senior princes who did not disclose its contents and asked her to find a safe place for it. Badriya did not mention the name of this prince but only told them that his name terrifies hearts. She had no choice but to do what he ordered. Badriya came in disguise in the dark and asked her mother to find a safe place because her mother's house would not raise suspicions as it had no connection to this prince. The mother told Badriya that nowhere was safer than the secret storage room in the wall of the well, so the three women cooperated in carrying that heavy sack to that room, which no one knew existed and could only be reached by lifting one of the stone steps. Badriya told them that while the Mamelukes began to send their harem and fortunes outside Cairo, they were preventing Egyptians from doing the same. Badriya left them before the call for the dawn prayer without anyone noticing after recommending that they too should go and find shelter while waiting for the disorder and turmoil to settle.

Outside their home, Cairo was in a state of confusion, bewilderment, and perplexity, filled with contradicting gossip. Most of al-Husseiniya's men went behind the barricades in Boulaq, while most of the women and children left the neighbourhood for safer places. Zainab's mother could not find a safe place for her family, so she decided to stay and face whatever would happen. Hours passed before the news arrived of the defeat of the Mamelukes and their flight to upper Egypt and the resulting chaos in the city. Then came the word of the massive fire in Boulaq and that the Franks were coming burning and killing everything in their path. The neighbourhood was struck with panic. At this point, Zainab's mother moved quickly, packing the few dinars she owned and some other belongings. She and Ali put Ahmed on the back of their donkey and rushed into the lane, She and Zainab followed behind them on foot with the dog trailing after them. The roads were crowded with thousands of fleeing Cairenes. No one helped anyone else, and everyone was trying to save himself. Everyone expected that the Franks were coming from the direction of Boulaq, so they fled to the south in the direction of the Old Cairo district. Around Zainab and her family were numerous fleeing families, each hoping to reach one of the safe villages in northern Upper Egypt. They were tired after hours of chaos without food or water; as if that was not bad enough, the news arrived from those who preceded them on this road saying that bandits of Arab Bedouins outside Cairo were blocking the road. They attacked everyone who came by, taking everything they carried down to their clothes, and killing anyone who tried to confront them.

Zainab stopped and looked at her mother for help and wondered with panic where they were to go now. She was stunned to see her mother sitting on the ground with her hands firmly grasping her chest and her face severely contracting in overwhelming pain, as the look of strength and determination in her eyes changed to misery and submission. Zainab asked her what was wrong. Her mother was silent, unable to respond, and had difficulty breathing.

In all situations, her mother was the one to guide her on what to do. Now she was alone at night among these vast fields. Here was Ahmad looking with alarm at their very sick mother on the ground without saying a word, and Ali stood in bewilderment behind him. On the one hand, the Franks were killing and burning everything in their way, and on the other hand the Arab Bedouins were harassing, looting, and killing everyone who fled. There was no way out of this grave catastrophe.

Zainab felt dizzy and staggered a few steps then sat on the muddy ground. Her mind was inundated with anguish, despair and gloom; she felt like she was falling into an abyss of darkness and loss and longed for death. Death appeared to her as an attractive smiling face or as a return home to her father's hugs after a long and arduous journey. She didn't know how long she had been in this state, and then a noise came; the voices of those around her came with good news: the Franks did not kill or burn anyone. The whole thing was just a rumor that stemmed from chaos and confusion. Now the crowd changed direction, everyone returned to their homes.

Zainab felt as if she was coming back to life, and she saw in her mind the image of alarm in her father's eyes as he looked at the paralysed Ahmed, which made her quickly rise, standing and determined. From now on, she would be the mother, surround Ahmed with her care at all costs, and bravely face whatever happened. She helped her mother get up, and the mother leaned on her arm. It wasn't long before the mother fell again, unable to move. Zainab decided to put her mother on the back of the donkey and ordered Ali to carry her brother Ahmed and continue the return journey. The road appeared long because of fatigue and hunger. When they finally reached home, Zainab put her mother to bed to find her lifeless. Her beloved mother was dead.

It happened on 1ˢᵗ August 1798

Abu Qir Bay, Alexandria

"Victory is not a word strong enough to describe what happened," said Nelson about the Battle of the Nile, also known as the Naval Battle of Abu Qir. Nelson must have been right as it was one of the most decisive battles in history. Between six o'clock in the evening of the first day of August and three in the afternoon the next day, the French fleet had been destroyed. There were more than five thousand French dead, and more than three thousand captured, while Nelson had lost no more than three hundred of his own men.

The French fleet commander, Vice-Admiral Brueys, anticipated Nelson's attack; however, he didn't build up his shore fortifications in good time so that the artillery could protect his fleet from the anticipated attack, nor did he send scout boats to provide early warning. When news arrived that Nelson's fleet had been spotted around five in the evening, some of his soldiers and engineers on Abu Qir Island were still busy building fortifications, and many sailors were helping them. Brueys did not go out to meet Nelson, thinking he would not start the attack before the morning, but he was wrong as Nelson had taken the unusual decision of starting the attack in the evening. Brueys placed his ships in a parallel row close to shore, believing that Nelson's ships could not reach the shallow water between his fleet and shore without the risk of becoming stranded, and he was wrong about this too. The shallow water turned out to be not that shallow, it was sufficient enough for Nelson's ships. Brueys should have anchored his ships closer to the shore. Nelson took advantage of this and began the attack by entering between the French fleet and the shore. He began bombarding the French vessels, but they could not respond as their guns were now uselessly pointing out to sea.

Unfortunately, that day, the large French flagship, L'Orient, which the Egyptians called the "half of the world", was being painted, and some flammable materials were left on deck. As a result, after the battle began, L'Orient caught fire and it spread rapidly. This ship was the greatest in the world at the time but no match for fire. It was the command ship, and it contained much ammunition and heavy guns that were brought for the campaign, as well as scientific devices and other equipment. When the quickly spreading fire reached the ammunition it caused an incredible legendary explosion that was heard miles away. Warriors on both sides froze for ten minutes, stunned by the massive sound and the bright flash. L'Orient, the pride of the French fleet, sank in its first naval battle and, with it, the dreams of the young commander Bonaparte. Of the seven hundred crew on board, only seventy survived.

Brueys did not live to witness the extent of the destruction that befell his fleet. He did not see the sinking and the capture of his ships one after the other because he was injured while he was in the command tower in L'Orient and lost his leg. He died two hours later of his injuries, one hour before the sinking of his ship.

General Kleber, who had remained in Alexandria to recover from injury, stood in the citadel of Alexandria watching from a distance as Nelson's ships approached the bay of Abu Qir and prepared for the attack. He was confident that Vice-Admiral Brueys could repel them, but this soon proved false. Darkness fell, and the battle continued, and he watched with sorrow as L'Orient exploded. The following day, he witnessed the horror of what was happening across the bay. France was without a fleet, and the French soldiers had become prisoners in Egypt. What a disaster. But as he was witnessing it from a distance, he was utterly unable to do anything.

Al-Salhiya, Egypt

Far from what was happening on the Mediterranean coast, Napoleon Bonaparte was chasing Ibrahim Bey in the Nile Delta region. After gaining total control of Alexandria and Cairo, the next step was to ensure this control was unchallenged. Those cunning mameluke princes refused to surrender, so he sent an army to follow Murad Bey in Upper Egypt and led another army to the east to hunt Ibrahim Bey.

After a long chase and many battles all the way from Cairo through the Delta to Sinai, Napoleon faced Ibrahim Bey's army several times. Each time, Ibrahim Bey managed to escape east, along with his followers, his harem, his wealth, and Bekir Pasha. Ibrahim Bey withdrew from the battle at al-Salhiya. Napoleon chased him again, reached the outskirts of the desert, clashed with the rear of his army and eliminated it, and thought that he had finally had Ibrahim Bey in his grip. But again his opponent slipped through his fingers and escaped deep into the desert, where it was impossible for Bonaparte to continue the pursuit.

He had hoped to capture Ibrahim Bey to secure undisputed power and the vast wealth he carried with him when he fled Cairo. It was now clear to him that he failed to achieve his goal after a long chase that cost him a lot of time, effort, and trouble. Now the French commander who conquered Europe felt like a failure. The young commander was unaware of what had become of his fleet in Abu Qir Bay, a battle that was perhaps the most decisive in ending his big dreams and might have changed world history. It might have been the first time he felt the sting of defeat, but it would not be the last.

Al-Sanadikya, Cairo

The friends gathered again for their evening get-together at Haj Mustafa's house after a break of several days. The chaos that happened when the French entered Cairo forced them to flee to safety, but now they were back and going on with life as before. Haj Mustafa lived his life with no greater aim than tranquillity and peace. He was wealthy and owned houses, other real estate, and controlled vast tracts of land. He had two wives and many children, servants, and slaves, and he would not engage in anything that could spoil his peace of mind, so he distanced himself from the conflicts between princes, imams, sheikhs, and Turks, satisfied with his life as it was. The pillars of his happy world had been severely shaken since the news of the arrival of the French fleet. He could protect himself and his family when chaos, looting, and vandalism occurred after the Mamelukes fled, leaving Cairo without a ruler or protection. An atmosphere of reassurance and relief prevailed when Napoleon, whom the Egyptians called Bonabarta or Sari Asker the Great, promised safety to the Cairenes. Still, suspicions and doubts remained even though on the surface things now appeared to go back to the way they were before, and his friends were back again over hookah and cups of coffee in the evening.

Mansour was the most troubled and suspicious attendee; Murad Bey's defeat befell him like a thunderbolt; he could never imagine that Murad Bey could be defeated; although Mansour was not surprised that Murad Bey fled the battle and then took his wealth, his harem, and his followers to Upper Egypt because Mansour knew that Murad Bey did not care about anything but himself. Mansour was keen to keep communication channels open between him and Murad Bey and continued to deliver the latest news to him. Still, now Mansour had to redo all his calculations as the French, or Francees as the Egyptians called them at that time, would kill anyone who contacted the Mameluke princes. He did not know to whom to give loyalty as so far, the conflict was still unresolved, and he would give his allegiance to whoever won. But until things became clear, he decided to show dedication to the French, the new masters of the country, while keeping his contact with Murad Bey secret. He knew for years how to hide his feelings; he did, despite his turmoil and alarm, seem to be the calmest of those present. When he talked, he sounded knowledgeable:

> 'The Francees took Cairo and promised safety to the people, and Sari Asker the great Bonabarta sent for the sheikhs and the leaders, and they came and agreed to appoint ten sheikhs to the new Diwan that will run Cairo. These sheikhs appointed the new governor and the chief of the police force from the Turks and Mamelukes who used to run Cairo before. Sari Asker the Great was amazed that the sheikhs had reappointed the Turks and the

Mamelukes, who despised and mistreated the Egyptians. Still, the sheikhs explained that al-ja'idiya and the lower classes could only be ruled by the Turks, as only the Turks could control them. Sari Askar accepted what the sheikhs wanted.'

'Sari Askar is well-intentioned and does not know much about al-ja'idiya; I cannot imagine how anyone but a Turk could restrain them.'

'The Francees seized the palaces of the Mameluke princes; Sari Asker took al-Alfi Bey's palace in al-Azbakeya; al-Alfi spent a considerable fortune preparing and refurbishing it with the most luxurious items, then came the Francees and took it before he moved in.'

'Security has not been established; people of the lower classes looted the palaces of Ibrahim Bey and Murad Bey, and burned them, and they looted several of the houses of other Mameluke princes. They took the mattresses, copper, and luggage and sold them at the lowest prices.'

'The Francees soldiers started this. They entered these houses to search for weapons or money and then left them open. They should have sealed and guarded them.'

'For us, there is nothing to fear. The Francees did nothing against the Egyptians and kept their word when they reassured people about their safety. Most French soldiers remained in their camps, and only some entered the city. They did not loot or sabotage, were nice and friendly to the Egyptians, and bought everything they needed at a higher price so that Egyptians felt at ease with them.'

'They could have taken everything they wanted from the people by force, but they didn't take anything without paying the full price, and they didn't ask anyone for work unless they paid for it. They didn't exploit or abuse people as the Mameluke princes did.'

'This communiqué they distributed to the people did not benefit them. Most Egyptians did not understand it, and those who did didn't find it convincing.'

'This is nothing but deception, such as claiming they are Muslims and protecting Islam when they are not. They do not disclose their real intentions to flatter the Egyptians because they anticipate the return of the Mamelukes to fight them again. They want to deceive the people until they take over the country and then destroy the religion of Islam.'

'They are using tricks and deception to get people to surrender and then they will show their true intentions.'

'Their real intentions are found in this communiqué, threatening that whoever resists them will be erased and not a trace of him will remain. This is their true purpose in sending that communiqué.'

The church

Priest Athanasius ended the service in the church after Mass by urging prayer and fasting and saying:

'"Do not be like the Pharisees whom Christ rebuked, saying, these people honour me with their lips, but their heart is far from me." Blessings come with prayer and supplication.'

Then he led everyone in prayer and concluded it, by saying:

'O Virgin, Mother of God Most High, the blessed, Queen of Angels, to whom do we turn for help? You alone are the mediator of all blessings; look at us and answer our prayers, hail Mary.'

Some Coptic Christians sat around Father Athanasius, discussing how things had turned out. Christian clerics used to lead the members of their sects and represent them before the Sultan and his deputies, from the governor to the Mameluke princes and the Turkish officers. They considered themselves responsible for their congregations and listened to their complaints just as the sheikhs did with Muslims. When the French arrived in Alexandria, the Copts and other Christians were subjected to looting and killing, so could the French now protect them? Attendees wondered:

> 'The Franks are from our religion, and they will support us and lift the injustice.'
>
> 'I'm afraid I have to disagree with that. We lived safely under the protection of the Sultan. The Mameluke princes and Turks are Muslims, so they do not interfere with our faith, while the Francees are Catholic Christians and will try to eliminate our Orthodox faith as the Crusaders tried.'

'There is no fear of that. They are not like the Crusaders and do not value Catholicism. We Christians were killed and suffered from looting before they arrived. The Christians have not been harmed since they took Cairo.'

'But they do value and regard Islam and try to get closer to Muslims. This is clear in the communiqué they sent, and we do not know anything about what they will do with Christians.'

Al-Husseiniya, district, Cairo

In a small mosque on the outskirts of al-Husseiniya, Hussein and his peers would come to pray and then attend Sheikh Abd al-Rahman lessons that followed the Isha prayer. This young sheikh had an influence and power among the lower classes, such as day labourers, street vendors, porters and others. They loved him because he appeared to understand them as if he was one of them, he understood their suffering and the injustice inflicted on them. He filed their complaints to the powerful and sometimes interceded for them with the police or Al Muhtasib. Hussein and his companions used to stay with him after Isha's prayer for the lesson and then to talk about matters of religion and worldliness; they admired his views and considered him their guide and role model. No one came to his lessons unless bearded, and he forbid them to smoke tobacco or hookah. He used to teach them about heresies and taboos that violated the Qur'an and Sunnah and the rules of Sharia, and he considered attending festivals and visiting the shrines of the righteous sheikhs to be heresies that Islam forbade and stressed not to do them. The talk that evening was about what the French had done since they took over Cairo:

'Praise be to Allah, and peace and blessings be upon the Messenger of Allah, his family and companions, and supporters.'

'There is no god but Allah, alone, and he has no partner; delusional are these Francees hypocrites, their term in the Egyptian country will not be long. When the message about them reaches the Sultan, he will bring his army to eliminate them; they cannot withstand the Sultan's army, the greatest in the world.'

'"God promised the hypocritical men and women and infidels the fire of hell in which they will remain forever, it is their judgement, and God cursed them, and they have a lasting torment". This is the truth of the great God.'

'This immoral communique that they distributed to the people is nothing but a deception for Muslims to overcome and humiliate them. They were lying when they said that they came to support the Sultan. It is unreasonable that the Sultan allowed infidels to enter the land of Muslims.'

'They say that all people are equal; how can they consider a Muslim equal to a non-Muslim? This is the worst blasphemy and heresy.'

'The laws of infidelity have plagued homes, and the rulings of infidelity prevailed over the provisions of Islam.'

'Every believer should fight against the enemies of God. Our enemies are corrupting religion and the world and must be stopped.'

'If the infidels begin to attack the sanctities of Muslims, then jihad well become obligatory for us. We must defend Islam, the religion of righteousness.'

Sheikh Abd al-Rahman stressed the need to prepare for jihad and advised them not to show hostility to the Franks publicly, but to collect all the weapons they could in secret.

The gathering broke up, and everyone got ready to go home. Hussein walked with Sheikh Abd al-Rahman on their way home to talk to him about the anguish in his heart and ask for advice as the sheikh knew of his love for Zainab. Hussein was on a date with Zainab and knew that he had to settle the matter that night. Zainab was strong-willed and would not accept any more procrastination or hesitation. He knew that if he did not meet with her soon as planned, it would be the end of their love.

In the darkness of the night and under the dim light of the oil lanterns in the narrow street. Hussein confessed that he still loved Zainab and wanted to marry her, but the difficulties started to mount since her mother began working with Badriya and since Zainab started to help her after the death of her father. Once Zainab became a singer in women's social gatherings, her family had become outcasts in the neighbourhood. Some would have expelled her from the area entirely, if it were not for their fear that Zainab's mother would complain to the Franks. Hussein's mother could not bear to hear the name Zainab or her mother at all, even though she used to love them. Hussein asked Zainab to leave her mother and marry him, and he would take her away from the neighbourhood, but she explained that she could not do that. She would not abandon her family when they needed her. Then Zainab's mother died, and Zainab was heard singing for French officers and not only in women's gatherings. Hussein still wanted to marry her and take her away from Badriya and from singing, but he feared the anger of his parents, especially his mother. If he did not face his family, he would lose Zainab forever.

Sheikh Abd al-Rahman listened patiently to everything he said and told him with firmness and certainty not to think about Zainab again and to immediately cut off all ties with her. He stressed that her departure, and that of her mother, from the traditions of decent families, was a kind of immorality, and that her actions were a departure from the Sharia. If her mother had raised her on the principles of religion, she would not have agreed to sing and would not have agreed to speak to Hussein alone. She was no longer virtuous Muslim woman. Sheikh Abd al-Rahman also advised Hussein to recite supplications and increase his reading of the Qu'ran. Sheikh Abd al-Rahman promised Hussein that he would find him a virtuous Muslim girl who would love him, be faithful to him, give him sons, and please his parents.

Hussein had no choice but to thank the Sheikh for his advice, but deep down, he was troubled by conflicting feelings. He felt sorrow and pain and wished that the Sheikh understood what was tormenting his soul, but at the same time, he was sure that Sheikh Abd al-Rahman was the one who knew the correct actions according to the law of God. Sheikh Abd al-Rahman went on his way, and Hussein remained alone in the narrow dark streets mulling things over in his mind until so much time had passed that he missed his date with Zainab. He returned home feeling sad and did not speak to anyone. In the light of the dim lamp in his room, he kept reading Qur'an from the Surat Taha and the Surat al-Falaq and Surat al-Nas, repeating their verses over and over. He went to bed and continued to recite the Suras saying verses: "Remember the name of your Lord and be most faithful to him", and "the mention of Allah reassures hearts", finally he repeated "Lay not on us a burden like that which You did lay on those before us (Jews and Christians); Allah, Put not on us a burden greater than we have the strength to bear. Pardon us and grant us forgiveness. Have mercy on us. You are our patron and give us victory over the disbelieving people". He finally calmed down and fell asleep until he heard the call to al-Fajr prayer coming from afar amid the silence. The muezzin said the familiar words, announcing that prayer was better than sleep. The Fajr prayer carried a divine magic that gave him peace. Hussein prayed alone, humbled and with tears streaming from his eyes, and felt consolation for his tormented soul.

Not far from Hussein, across the alley in Zainab's house, she was still lying in bed, in tears, when she heard the call for dawn prayers. Another day of grief and misery, she hadn't slept all night, and she had much work to do with Badriya that day. She could bear the fatigue and lack of sleep, but what really hurt her was the massive emptiness she felt now that she had decided to forget Hussein forever. Although she hadn't spoken to him much recently, he was the partner of her sweet childhood memories and the man of her dreams as a teenager. It wasn't easy for her to forget him, but that's precisely what she had to do. He broke his promise and left her alone, waiting for him in the dark, hoping that he would somehow find a way to fulfil her dream of marriage. He abandoned her and left her alone, just as his family had abandoned her mother after a lifetime of friendship. She saw this as unforgivable treachery. Yes, she must forget Hussein forever and not give in to feelings of sorrow. She had much hard work ahead of her that day, and she had to do it the best she could.

Al-Azbakeya district, Cairo

No one in Cairo knew what was happening in Abu Qir Bay. In a quiet garden overlooking al-Azbakeya pond, Julien's friends gathered under a grape arbour as they had since their arrival in Cairo. The garden was part of one of the palaces of the fleeing princes in which the members of the scientific expedition resided after Bonaparte's capture of Cairo. The young scientists had no military duties and were dedicated to scientific research, each in his field. They met in the evenings and often preferred this quiet place to the noisy parties at the officers' mess because this was also where they met others they had befriended in Cairo. One of these Cairenes was Raymond, a distant cousin of Julien, who was born in Cairo, the son of a French merchant who lived for several decades. Another was Michael, the son of a Greek Christian merchant who also settled al-Muski neighbourhood. This was where European merchants had lived since the days of Saladin. Because of this friendship, Julien learned more of the Arabic dialect spoken by the man on the street in Cairo. He was the one who mingled with the Egyptians the most, and soon he could conduct a dialogue with them without the help of an interpreter.

The scientific expedition had not had a happy start because one of the fleet ships carrying their scientific equipment hit a shoal and sank when they began to go ashore in Abu Qir Bay. The friends did not find much of interest in Alexandria; though they had followed the Rosetta Road when Julian and the other half of the army had followed the commander Bonaparte down the desert road. While Julien was hungry and in danger of dying from the scorching sun, hot sand and lack of water, his friends had much good food and fresh water in Rosetta. They found a lot in that city to attract their attention, so they immediately began their work studying, researching and collecting samples. Since they arrived in Cairo, they had been staying in the luxurious palace of the former prince. They immediately began to work hard, as long as there was daylight, to help create the scientific institute project, that would be the centre of their studies in Egypt.

The initial Egyptians' fear of the French disappeared, and the friends saw nothing but affection and warmth from them, so after completing the day's hard work, the friends loved to wander around the markets of Cairo and talk to regular people. The friends' chat that evening was about Egypt, Cairo, and the Cairenes:

'Our skins are burned by the scorching sun. The Egyptians are protected by their dark skin.'

'A cool night breeze with a glass of good wine refreshes the soul after hard work in the day's stifling heat.'

'The colloquial language that people speak in the market is easy to learn; Egyptians say things clearly, and it is easier to understand than the language of the sheikhs.'

'Egyptians express their thoughts not just by talking as they combine talking with movements of the face, head and hands, using expressive movements like pantomime that can be understood without words.'

'I learned a lot from repeating words and being associated with the situation; I learned Asalamo alykum, peace be with you, bakshish, tips, yasaater, god forbid, insha'a alla, god willing, alhamdulillah, thanks to god and yela'anabook, a swear word. This word confused me, Sometimes it is said in anger, and sometimes to be humorous.'

'It's two words, meaning God curse your father.'

'I like the word Ma'alish, never mind or do not worry. It is quite often said on various occasions; it summarises the philosophy of the Egyptians.'

'The eye language shows that the Egyptians are kind and noble at heart.

'I like the food and drink in the market. Very colourful, vibrant vendors serve sharbat, carob, and liquorice drinks. The taste of fresh cold water from the pottery pot they call al-kulla is really nice.'

'Al-Sakka was carrying his goat skin bag selling fresh water.'

'The Egyptians are skilled in cooking chicken and roasted pigeons with freekeh, okra and mulukhiyah. The taste of their bread is lovely.'

'I enjoy this great pastry with honey and the sweets they make with pistachios, hazelnuts and almonds.'

'The fresh fruits are great; I love their apricots, figs and melons.'

'I was shocked to see so many blind people in this city.'

'You can link this to seeing many children with pus-filled eyes. That must be why there are so many blind people around. Our doctors must work to find out more about this eye disease.'

'Egyptians think the reason is the evil eye, which is the gaze of a grudging person that has the power to harm. They believe that wearing a blue bead protects them.'

'They are intensely superstitious and believe in myths. Copts believe in miracles of the saints, and Muslims believe in miracles of the righteous sheikhs. They swear these miracles are true and talk about the many witnesses who saw them.'

'Someone offered to make me an amulet.'

'You can't differentiate between Muslim and Christian in appearance, but they always refer to each other by religion.'

'You divide people in Europe according to their nationalities, but the Egyptians divide people according to their religions.'

On another side of al-Azbakeya, Badriya stood in the restaurant which she called the food house facing the pond waiting for Zainab; Unusually Zainab was late. They had much work to do before the French came in the evening.

Since the death of Zainab's mother, Badriya treated her as her daughter and considered herself responsible for her and her brother. Badriya's life had changed since the arrival of the French in Cairo. After a wave of fear, unruliness, and chaos, things settled down nicely. She saw nothing of the French except warmth and friendly manners. Her trade boomed when she found that thousands of soldiers and officers were going to the markets looking for food, drink, and other necessities, and she knew exactly where to find everything they needed. They paid generously, treated women with respect and decency, and didn't treat her as a lower class person or look down on her as she was being treated by Egyptian men.

She noticed that the settled Egyptian Christians of European origin had established houses to make food and drinks in the French style to satisfy the needs of the French in Cairo. The concept of such food houses or restaurants was unknown to her. She knew where to find the best chicken, pigeons, fish, and meat and where to find good wine, honey, sugar, soap and all the needs of these food houses, so she worked first with them. She saw in this the opportunity to make money and climb out of poverty, so she hurried and mortgaged everything she and Zainab owned to buy themselves a café facing al-Azbakeya pond from one of al-Arwam, the Greek Christians, and she turned it into a house of food similar to what she saw in the others that has spring up. She put a sign on the door in French, bought more wooden tables and chairs, divided the place into sections based on whether the prices were cheap, expensive or somewhere in between, and marked each section with the number of dirhams or francs to be paid. She brought cooks, servers and porters to serve her customers and brought musical instruments and musicians to entertain them. Zainab helped her in the morning and sang in the evening while Badriya supervised the preparation and serving of food.

On the way to meet Badriya, Zainab stopped at the shrine of al-Hussein, the grandson of the prophet, repeating the supplications that she had memorised since her childhood. She no longer prayed the five prayers and no longer read the Qur'an as she did before, but she still sometimes prayed to God and loved the Prophet Muhammad and his family and asked for their intercession, and used to ask for intercession the righteous Sheikhs, She also prayed and asked for help from the Virgin Mary, she took from her mother the sanctification of the Virgin Mary, the mother of Issa (Jesus). She heard from her mother about the many blessings of the Virgin Mary on both Christians and Muslims. She saw Ahmed's illness was worsening day by day and the paralysis was spreading in his body relentlessly. It seemed clear to her that he was slowly dying and that he would not live long, but in her heart still had a glimmer of hope that a miracle might happen. All her prayers to God were centred around Ahmed, but that day she went to al-Hussein's shrine to ask for help and solace for her own soul. She had been inundated with sadness, sorrow and disappointment since Hussein missed his date with her and left her waiting, crying alone in the dark.

Her unwillingness to pray regularly was caused by her hate for the hypocrisy of many worshippers. She used to see many men praying the five prayers every day, not stopping recitations from Qur'an and hadith, and not leaving the rosary; clicking prayer beads between their fingers. Yet, they also paid and received bribes, and their behaviour was characterised by injustice, lying, deception and falseness. They even swore to God to justify lying. She saw many women who pretended to be virtuous, and never missed a prayer, appearing to follow all fundamental practices of

Islam, and repeated litanies. Yet, they also desperately chased Badriya to find an intermediary who could contact demons and evil spirits to subdue their unruly husband or to inflict harm on another of his wives. They were the ones who made her an outcast from the neighbourhood because of her work with the French. Zainab despised hypocrisy. Badriya shared this view with her and often told her not to try to contact Hussein and to forget him completely. Zainab wished she had listened to this advice. After a long day of hard work, she sat exhausted, talking to Badriya and telling her that Hussein had missed the crucial date with her. She expected Badriya to blame her for not listening. But Badriya did not do any of this. She just embraced her as a mother would, and comforted her.

It happened in September 1798

Al-Azbakeya district, Cairo

The French officers loved the food, drink, and music in the restaurant run by Badriya. The place became crowded every night with French officers and soldiers and the French franks and dirhams flowed in, but the work was hard. It was not easy for a woman to manage such a business in the world of men. She needed more assistants, servers, and cooks, but she also had to economise to pay off her debts. The daylight hours did not seem enough to finish everything that needed to be done; buying the ingredients and the drinks needed, arguing and haggling with merchants all the time about their prices, and then the long hours in the kitchen with the cooks and kitchen porters, preparing the food and tables. Zainab shared the workload with Badriya for most of the day and then left her to prepare with the musicians in the evening.

Zainab worked hard despite her preoccupation with the affairs of her home and her sick brother Ahmed.

Zainab learned a lot from Badriya. She learned to be strong and decisive and to take the initiative to straighten things out in dealing with merchants, workers and cooks. But in the evenings she also learned to be friendly with the French, the source of dirhams and francs. It was challenging for a woman to do such work. She knew from a young age that she was beautiful and attractive. The admiration of people around her, wherever she went, satisfied her pride, but she did not feel comfortable with the way most men looked at her, undressing her with their eyes. She hated such crudeness. Many men saw women as mere pleasures to be had, which caused her great difficulty in her hard work. She liked the French because they treated women with appreciation and respect and always spoke to her kindly. She learned French to be able to talk to them and loved it. She also very much admired the changes they brought about in Cairo and saw them as more knowledgeable and advanced than the Egyptians. She heard about French doctors and modern medicine, and she wished to find the opportunity to take her brother Ahmed to be seen by one of them so that they might find a cure for him. As it happened with the Egyptian audiences, the French audiences praised her singing and she noticed that many French people sought to talk to her afterwards.

At the dining house, Zainab met Julien and his friends, who liked the food and often came for dinner. Zainab spoke to them in French and noticed that Julien seemed very interested in her. She knew that some French soldiers were seeking women for sex, so she was keen to make it clear to everyone that she was not that sort of girl and strongly repelled anything other than an attempt at a short conversation. She loved singing in the evening as it gave her pleasure and comfort after the day's hard work, even if she had to face these men who wanted more than singing from her. That night she sang an old Egyptian muwashshah:

> "You whom wine played with, how lovely are these features
> Joyful like drunk shakes with fondness, like a branch moves and bends with the breeze"

Again, Julien stopped her and told her that her voice was sweet, smooth, and gentle, and he said to her that although he spoke Arabic, he could not understand the songs and asked her to translate for him. She said that it was about a man who flirts with his lover, but she was not fluent enough in French to translate it for him in a way to feel the tenderness and ingenuity of the poet. She was confused about what this Frenchman really wanted from her.

One day, Badriya told her that the prince, who had left some of his fortunes with her before fleeing Cairo, had been killed in upper Egypt with some of his followers. He had no descendants, and she believed no one knew about the belongings that had been left with her. They went to Zainab's house in al-Husseiniya and waited until everyone went to sleep and then went together to look at what the prince had left. By the dim light of the lamp, took out the burlap sack they had left inside the well's hidden room. Badriya opened the sack to see what was in it, they found some pistols, gunpowder, and daggers, but they also found a bag full of gold dinars. Badriya gasped with surprise and said it was a tremendous fortune that God had placed in their hands. Badriya took about half of the gold dinars, left everything as it was, and locked the room.

Badriya paid their debts and hired more workers and cooks to help them run the restaurant. These gold dinars that came down from heaven changed Zainab's life. She was now able to reward Ali for his dedicated service to her brother by buying him a Nubian slave girl whom Ali himself chose to be his wife. This girl also helped Zainab manage the house, which relieved her of much daily hard work. She felt as if life was smiling at her now after a period of gloom and a long frown.

Napoleon Bonaparte sat in the great al-Azbakeya palace, the "citizen general", as the French called him or "Sari Askar the Great", as the Egyptians called him. He reviewed how things were going in Cairo with his aides. He had in mind the events of this disastrous day when he was on his way back returning from al-Salihiya after chasing Ibrahim Bey. When he arrived in Belbeis, he received the horrific news of the destruction of his fleet in Abu Qir. He was stunned and felt as if the earth was shaking, the news was such a severe blow to his dreams. But he was a leader and was destined to lead and not show weakness. His soldiers were rejoicing in their victory over the Mamelukes, unaware, and he then said to them "Rejoice, it seems that you love this country, be delighted, and strive to get used to the weather here, as we have become without a fleet that could take us back to

France." Their hearts were troubled, but he reassured them that they were self-sufficient and did not need aid from France, that Egypt was full of resources, and that they would find everything they needed.

The next step was to change all his plans. He had been commissioned to come to Egypt to study the possibility of a permanent French colony in there and to return within six months. This had now changed to a long-term stay in Egypt, but that did not preclude the possibility of starting from Egypt to the Levant and from there to India, just as Alexander the Great did and just as he planned before the fleet was destroyed.

He has achieved a lot so far. He convinced Egyptians that he was not Louis IX, that he did not seek to Christianize them like the Crusaders, and that he was a supporter of Islam; he spent a lot of effort, time, and money in the celebrations of the Nile festival and the Prophet Mohamed's birthday and in protecting the Hajj caravans. The Diwan was established in Cairo and the provinces, and the ulema were convinced to participate in the country's administration. Those ulema, sheikhs, Turks and what remained of the Mamelukes collaborated with him and became part of his French regime. The Scientific Institute, with its various departments, was established: mathematics, nature, economics, politics and arts to become the Egyptian Institute, similar to the French Institute. His scientists introduced new methods of milling wheat, making bread and beer, purifying drinking water and making gunpowder, and his doctors built modern hospitals; he introduced a new system of education, postal services, cleaning the streets by sweeping and spraying, lighting the streets at night, and removing the doors between neighbourhoods to ensure security and prevent looting and theft. He renewed and established buildings and fortifications. He planned to develop an efficient tax collection system. He introduced several laws on birth and death registration and inheritance laws and laws to limit the spread of the plague epidemic. A new legal system was set up based on a Sharia Court made up of Al-Azhar sheikhs and a general court adjudicating matters of trade and tax formed by six Muslim merchants and six Copts headed by a Coptic named Malti. The Copts are the ones who know about accounting and commercial matters. He also introduced printing to Egypt, and the newspaper Al-Tanbeeh was distributed to Egyptians to introduce them to the new ways of running the country. These developments have become well-established, and he is now in full control. French scientists' efficiency and competence and the well-organized French administrative apparatus guaranteed an extended and stable stay for the French in Egypt.

Nasiriyah Lane, Al Darb Al Gadeed, Cairo:

Julien met his French friends at their workplace at the end of a day of work and admired the library and scientific institute's construction, and felt like the place was part of France; these young scientists had accomplished a lot in a short period. Then they all made their way to dinner at Zainab and Badriya restaurant. The conversation between friends was about their work at the Scientific Institute. They talked about visiting the pyramids and specially about the Great Pyramid, the highest and largest building in the world. They also talked about the news that came from their friends in the scientific mission who accompanied the campaign of General Desaix to Upper Egypt to pursue the fugitive Prince Murad Bey. From them they heard stories of magnificent temples and tombs, marvelous statues and exquisite inscriptions on the walls believed to be in an ancient language that told the history of a great civilisation, depicting the kings and queens of the past.

The friends debated whether modern Egyptians were the descendants of this civilisation of the distant past. One of them thought it was difficult to imagine that "these ignorant fanatics" were descendants of the people who made this great civilisation. He suggested that perhaps those who made this civilisation perished for some reason and were replaced by the ancestors of the current Egyptians. The opinion of another was that the Egyptians of today were no worse off than the medieval French and that they too could restore civilisation to their country as was done in Europe. Opinions differed, and the argument continued, but Julien's mind was far away from the discussion. He hasn't stopped thinking about Zainab since he first saw her singing, surrounded by admiration. Her beautiful face, sweet soft voice, charming personality, and intelligence were very much attractive. He found pleasure in talking to her, but for some reason, she seemed unwilling to spend much time with him.

Al-Husseiniya district, Cairo

It was the calm before the storm. Feelings of anger, indignation, resentment and hatred flowed from every side, just as the wind flows from every side as a storm forms and grows. The effects of the execution of Muhammad Kurayyim, the governor of Alexandria, raised a sense of anger and antipathy among the public, it was true that he had tried to confront the French when they arrived in Alexandria, but he later surrendered, and Bonaparte, asked him to continue as governor when he accepted submission and loyalty to the French. But when the French arrived in Cairo, they found a letter from him to Murad Bey calling on him to fight the French and trying to reduce and trivialize their power and control, Bonaparte considered this as a betrayal and breach of his trust and so issued an order on the execution of Muhammad Kurayyim by firing squad, and the confiscation of his property and money, unless he paid a ransom of thirty thousand Riyal Fransah which were the French francs in the Egyptian dialect. He had to pay within twenty-four hours to save his life. Kurayyim could not pay and so the sentence was carried out by firing squad followed by cutting off his head and parading it through the streets, with it went a town crier shouting "this is the penalty for those who contact the Mamelukes."

In the light of this, Sheikh Abd al-Rahman invited all the mujahideen brothers to wait in the mosque after the Isha prayer and then began his speech:

'The Franks, the infidels, killed Sayyid Muhammad Kurayyim because he did not pay the ransom. Still, he challenged them with the courage of the Mujahideen. He said to the infidel Bonabarta: if it was his destiny to die, paying the ransom wouldn't spare him from death, and if it was his destiny to live, then why should he pay? Allah the Almighty says in His Holy Book "those who believe are fighting for the sake of Allah and those who disbelieve are fighting for the sake of the tyrant so fight the followers of Satan, as the deception of Satan is weak." True are the words of Almighty God and Almighty God also says "Fight those who do not believe in Allah or the day of judgement and do not forbid what is forbidden by Allah and His Messenger and don't take the religion of righteousness." True are the words of Almighty God. Al-Bukhari narrated from the hadith of Ibn 'Umar that the Messenger of Allah, peace and blessings of Allah be upon him, said: "I was commanded to fight the people until they testified that there is no God but Allah and that

Muhammad is the Messenger of Allah." It is now the time for jihad.'

'Our jihad is with the sword and the spear against the Franks and the Christians. Whoever calls for a faith other than Islam is our enemy.'

'This is a malicious campaign, those deceivers who falsely claim to support Islam are nothing but arrogant people who do not understand Islam. They are corrupt and immoral. Muslims are the righteous and the people of goodness.'

'Bonabarta is an infidel who leads an army of infidels and encourages Christians at the expense of Muslims.'

'They seek to elevate the Christians. Christians preside over Muslims. They made Malti the Coptic infidel head of the General Court, and he is helped by Christians who argue with Muslims in their laws; they want equality in inheritance between females and males, this is clearly contrary to the text of the Holy Qur'an'

'The infidel Christians seized the endowments organisation and cut the salaries of jurists, blind people, muezzins, imams and those who deserved to be served by endowments.'

'Christians gloat at Muslims and seek to tease them by wearing cashmere and white turbans and riding mules.'

'Bonabarta took the doors off of lanes in all the neighbourhoods because he plans to kill Muslims while they are at Friday prayers.'

'They transgress in public with no shame, dancers and alcohol are in the officers' mess, and immoral acts in cafés are contrary to Sharia law.'

'Their women pass in the streets with unveiled faces, and servants give way to them like princesses; the purity is in the veiled face. The liberation of women is decadence.'

'Egyptians are dying of rage from this lack of decency. French soldiers enter ladies' houses, that even the Pasha himself would not dare to enter. Bonabarta has allowed his men to enter these ladies' homes under the pretext of searching.'

'The excuse of searching is a ploy to loot houses.'

'They show off their soldiers in uniforms in military parades on the birthday of the prophet and during the festival of the Nile to show their power and humiliate Muslims.'

'They demolish mosques under the pretext of building fortifications and vandalise graveyards under the guise of fighting the plague. Their purpose is nothing but to humiliate Muslims.'

Hussein shared their sense of anger, and of their sanctity being violated. The French scandalous acts were nothing less than insults! Still, he wondered about Sheikh Abd al-Rahman description of Muhammad Kurayyim's courage, because he had heard from his father a different story in which there was no courage. His father said that Kurayyim sent a message to the sheikhs asking them to pay his ransom and pleaded with them saying desperately "Buy me, O Muslims", but they had nothing to redeem him with because everyone was worried about themselves and what calamity might befall them next. Hussein was also sorry for what was said about the Christians. He understood the reasons people were angry at the Franks, but he did not know the reason why they hated the Christians; many of whom he had known since childhood and did not see in them anything of what the Brotherhoods said. Yet he was certain that Sheikh Abd al-Rahman was the one who knew the true religion and how to achieve the common good of Muslims. He felt distressed whenever he heard about Zainab being described by people as loose and unashamed. He knew that she sang for French officers, an unforgivable moral corruption, but he deep inside he was still in love with her and wished he had not abandoned her. He wondered if one day she could be returned to the true religion and become a faithful Muslim again.

The church

The unrest had ceased in Cairo, and Christians felt safe, going and coming as they used to do before. Some of them stayed to speak to each other after Sunday Mass and the departure of Father Athanasius:

'Bonabarta persecutes Christians to please Muslims.'

'Bonabarta does not care about religion, whether Christianity or Islam; he cares only about governance. He stands for justice and equality because he allows Christians to carry weapons, ride mules and horses, put turbans on their heads and wear whatever clothes they want, precisely like Muslims.'

'But Christians should be careful when appearing in the streets and markets in clothes that were forbidden to them in the days of the Mamelukes because Egyptians are not used to that.'

'The Christians were initially happy with the Francees and then realised that life under the Mamelukes was better; I wouldn't say I liked these new systems and interference in people's privacy.'

'We had more freedom under the Mamelukes, the Francees forbid people from speaking out, and they ordered the tongues cut out of two Syrian Christians and a Muslim for talking about what happened to the French fleet in Abu Qir. They could only escape punishment if they paid a fine of one hundred riyals each. Everyone could see that they had not committed a crime.'

'The Francees did not take the fines they demanded after all; when the sheikhs collected the money to save the men, the French governor pardoned them and returned the money to the sheikhs to be given to charity.'

Al-Sanadikya district, Cairo

Serenity and peace returned to the assembly of friends in the house of Haj Mustafa and also returned were the sarcasm, jokes and loud laughter, but even though doubt, suspicion and uncertainty still lurked within. Mansour was the most suspicious and bewildered of them all, thoughts swirling in his head. He realized that he needed to decide to whom to offer his services and loyalty. Power, influence and authority are all in the hands of Bonaparte, Sari Askar the Great. He tried many ways to approach him directly, but he could not manage it. Instead, he approached many of Bonaparte's aides and provided them with information. He told them what people said about the French, what actions the sheikhs were taking in public, and specially what they were doing in secret. He gained their trust and became close to them, so close that they asked him for advice in dealing with the Egyptians. Two prominent sheikhs were part of this assembly of friends. Sheikh Ismail was peaceful by nature and friendly to all, avoiding disputes and quarrels, but Sheikh Abdul Ghani was, on the contrary, puritanical in his beliefs, vocal in his opinions and not afraid to speak his mind loudly. Mansour did not feel safe with the French because he doubted their ability to survive and believed that the Sultan's army would soon come to eliminate them. Mansour left his concerns aside and shared in the talk about current affairs:

'These cunning people claim to love Islam; their logic is that Egyptians live by faith, so they will rule us by faith. It is so devious that they show respect for religious rites, celebrating the birth of the Prophet and protecting the Hajj, to the degree that their chief even took off his military jacket and entered the dhikr circle with the Muslims.'

'No Egyptian believes his claim of love for Islam. It has only caused people to be wary of the French since they did not love religion distinctive from their religion except to get closer to Egyptians for their own plan. Look what they did to Mohammed Kurayyim; they killed him and paraded his head in the streets.'

'Don't blame Bonabarta; Muhammad Kurayyim betrayed his agreement with the Francees.'

'The Francees are untrustworthy, yet their weapons, science and studies are superior and admirable. Their chief, Bonabarta is shrewd and possesses a deep knowledge of history, and he has respect for the sheikhs of al-Azhar and reverence for their knowledge as well.'

'Showing their superiority in science and knowledge and displaying their power and might is nothing but a way to humiliate Muslims.'

'While they were showing off their superiority, one of the sheikhs challenged them to make him appear in Cairo and Morocco simultaneously, but they could not.'

'A man cannot be in two different places at the same time.'

'This is nonsense, it happened, and it is a proven fact that cannot be questioned, many witnesses testified that one righteous Sheikh was present in Cairo and Mecca at the same time. The Francees with all their knowledge cannot achieve this.'

'They violate the sanctity of homes by examining and searching under the pretext of preventing the epidemic. How does inspection prevent an epidemic?'

'The Francees's scientists and physicians have a great deal of skill and knowledge and have recommended it. Inspections are only meant to protect themselves and Egyptians from the plague. They have prevented people from burying the dead in graveyards near their dwellings and recommended burying them in faraway deep pits instead. They have called for hanging laundry, and mattresses on the roofs for several days and fumigating houses. They stressed the need to report the sick to them, so that they could sent a doctor to examine them and determine if the disease was the plague. All this is to protect people from the spread of the epidemic. That's what their doctors recommended.'

'People are angry, fed up, and full of complaints, and anger is everywhere. The Francees said that they came to free us from the injustice of the Mamelukes, but they have simply imposed another form of injustice on us. Forcing the registration of births, marriages, and deaths and making people pay a fee to do it, is a nuisance, harassment, and an assault on people's freedom. The street lighting system is a senseless extravagance and a waste. One lamp is enough for every place; there need not be a lamp for every house or for the lighting to last all night. Removing the walls and the doors of the lanes has frightened people, so they have closed their shops and markets.'

'The Francees organise the affairs of the state according to their own ways and what they are accustomed to in their country, but this is nothing less than a regime change on Egyptians.'

'Many people have seen them search houses for the Mamelukes' money. They took everything left by them. They even executed several men caught stealing or dealing in goods stolen from the Mamelukes and imposed heavy fines on others.'

'The marriage of some Franks to the daughters of Egyptian notables took place after their sham conversion to Islam. The recitation of the two testimonies alone is not enough to make a person a Muslim.'

'What about Franks submitting to women and spending on them generously?'

'They want women to be treated with appreciation and men to treat their wives respectfully.'

'This is an invasion of the minds and thoughts of Muslims. The demise of their state is near, the

Sultan's army is on the way and will eliminate them.'

The differences in opinion between the men were the same as ever, but none of the attendees did not believe that the Egyptians were eager to be liberated from the Franks.

It happened on 21st October 1798

"When that (the bombs) fell on them, and they saw it, and they have never seen it before,

they shouted ya salaam from these alaam , (meaning ooh, what are all these pains!), God of hidden kindness save us from what we fear!

And they ran away from every market and got into the clefts.

And the throwing (bombing)continued from the castle and the Kiman until the pillars were shaken.

And destroyed in its passage the walls of the houses and fell in some palaces

And descended down to the homes and agents and deafened the ears with its tremendous sound"

Abd al-Rahman Bin Hassan al-Jabarti

From the book "Wonders of Antiquities in Biographies and News"

Cairo, 1798

Al-Husseiniya district, Cairo

'Father, father, father; what is this, what is this, father?'

The sounds of shocking horrific explosions, dust obscuring vision, flames spread far, through the city, there was the pungent stench of gunpowder, screams and howling came from every direction, there were thunderous deafening noises, and the sounds of doors shattering and stones slamming into each other. Among all that horror and noise, Hussein was able to discern the voice of his younger brother Mustafa screaming repeatedly:

'What's this, father? What's this sound, father?'

Mustafa held firmly onto his father's robes while his mother held the youngster's hand. Mustafa, a six-year-old boy, shouted to his father, but his father couldn't answer. The father's face was rigid with horror, surprise and confusion. The little one was used to getting the answer to every question from his father, but this time he was horrified to find his father's face frozen and his body motionless. Mustafa screamed in terror and then returned to ask him again desperately.

'Father, father, what's this sound?'

Hussein also sought help from his father, as he had always relied on his father's wisdom and knowledge, but not this time. He had just heard the shocking sound of the huge and appalling explosions before he realized what they were. The sound of explosions continued incessantly, each time a huge reverberation, followed by the sounds of walls and ceilings collapsing, screaming, howling, and ululating. Scattering stones, and dust produced stifling suffocating odours. It became difficult for him to breathe. He looked around through the thick smoke and flames and was horrified to see the house's front wall had collapsed. The earth was quaking with terrifying sounds as if it had been ravaged by a tornado from the sky. The neighbourhood suddenly turned into a battlefield. Shops and homes were destroyed and many people around disappeared under the rubble. Tremendous voices, the likes of which no one has ever heard. Bright flashes and black stones descend from the sky and a blazing, burning wind slapped his face. He closed his eyes and fell to the ground. His father was just steps away. In the short time between each explosion, the father saw his wife's unveiled face rigidly terrified as the faces of others with confusion and bewilderment. Children's screams remained unanswered. The clatter of rolling stones was heard like the echo in the bellies of the mountains, the sound of walls collapsing like the roar of ferocious beasts. Their ears were filled with the sound of running animals that couldn't be seen and the cries of terrified dogs whose barking sounded like wailing.

For a while, Haj Ibrahim did not know what to do or where to go, but soon his survival instincts took over, so he pushed his wife and children quickly behind the big strongly solid built mud oven, and they all lay on the ground with their heads buried in their hands and their hearts trembling and beating loudly, waiting for God's judgment. The explosions were flowing, the ground beneath them was shaking, and the furniture was flying around them, all of which melted them from fear. With the sound of explosions and screaming and crying around them, they were mumbling litanies and verses from the Qur'an:

> 'There is no God but Allah, Muhammad is the messenger of Allah.'
>
> 'Glory be to him who has in his hand the kingdom of all things, and to him, you shall return.'
>
> 'Oh God, make us die Muslims and revive us Muslims and make us join the righteous. Oh God, I ask you for forgiveness. Oh God, cover our faults and relieve our fears.'
>
> 'Oh Allah, I seek refuge in you from the bad fate, remove from us all evil, calamity and affliction, and keep us away from the evil of destiny.'

Not far away, Zainab had come in the morning to be with her brother Ahmed to check on his safety amid the grave events around them. On her way home, she saw young men gathered in the neighbourhood behind barricades. They carried sticks, pipes and knives in their hands, but that did not give her a sense of security. Suddenly, the ground shook beneath them, and substantial successive explosions began to knock people to the ground. She saw nothing but dust, destruction, and shattered utensils scattered around them. She saw someone flying through the air and falling, injuring his head as he struck the wall. She was terrified; she had never heard an explosion of that magnitude before; it appeared as if it was the Doomsday in al-Husseiniya, as if the earth shook and the sky fell on it. She ran home and hurried to carry her brother and quickly ran towards the well in the backyard, followed by the dog and the Nubian slave Ali. She went down several steps to take shelter in the walls of the well and hugged her brother tightly. She hoped that the waterless well would be a safe shelter, but the enormous sounds followed, and with it, the shaking of the earth and it seemed as if the walls of the well might collapse and bury them all in the ground. She realised that there was nothing else she could do. Her brother did not say a word, but she noticed the horror in his eyes and the trembling of his body; her father's face flashed in her imagination with alarm as he saw Ahmed trembling. She closed her eyes, recited the two testimonies, and resigned herself to what fate might bring.

She did not know how long it had been. She thought this immense ordeal would never end. Eventually, she noticed that the horrific noises had subsided and that the sounds of screaming and wailing had changed and became something more like the noise caused by the arrival of good news. She ordered Ali not to move and went out to see what had happened. Most of the walls of her house seemed intact, and so next she rushed out into the neighbourhood. She realised that the massive explosions were the bombs that came from the cannons of the French in the castle, and then came the good news that Sari Askar of the French had ordered a halt to the bombing.

She was in great agony at the horror of what she saw in the neighbourhood. The resulting destruction was indescribable; no house was spared from damage, unbelievable destruction. After the black smoke and dust started to clear, the streets and the lanes appeared in horrific ruins. Entire buildings were lost, the roads were full of pieces of glass and scattered stones. There were bodies of the dead and wounded everywhere. Some were trapped inside the rubble, some were torn to pieces between the walls. There was blood flowing in the streets, and trees that had collapsed. She couldn't believe that one day she would live to see this destruction around the neighbourhood and see all these dead on the roads, all these burdened with the pain of their wounds, and the separation of loved ones. When the bombing stopped the sounds of screaming, wailing, ululating covered all other noises. All around, people repeated the phrase "we belong to God and to Him we return." Nothing like this had ever been seen before. She felt heartbroken for the disaster that hit the people and the neighbourhood and for all the devastation that she saw everywhere.

Many of the dead were people whom she knew. She worked with many men and women to clear the rubble and extricate those people who remained trapped yet still alive. Not far from her home, she noticed a scarf she knew well among the ruins. She hurried and removed some wood and stones to find Badriya's face: pale, expressionless, soaked in a pool of blood, lifeless. Zainab fainted and fell in a state of semi-consciousness. She felt like the ground beneath her was shaking again. An overwhelming feeling of despair, sadness and regret swept over her when she saw Badriya-always so funny, playful, and full of life- now a helpless corpse in front of her. When she lost her father and mother, Badriya was her second mother. Now she was truly an orphan. Badriya had lived in al-Azbakeya and she did not expect to find her in this devastated, shattered place. Badriya might have come to al-Husseiniya to check on her aunt, who lived there, and because of her bad fortune, she was caught in the bombardment and could not return. Zainab sat on the ground, muddled, not knowing what to do; she felt that the air she was breathing was too heavy. Her feelings froze, and she couldn't even cry. She remained perplexed in place, not moving. Things got mixed up in her mind, and she seemed unable to grasp the events around her.

She noticed that people had begun to come out of their hiding places, and the neighborhood became crowded. The noise rose again, many people shouting and screaming in search of their loved ones, many wailing and ululating, and women were slapping their cheeks and throwing dust on their heads in grief. She heard some people talking to her, but she didn't answer. Then she remembered the looks of strength and firmness in her mother's eyes and woke up from her dismal rhapsody. This was not the time for weakness and dithering. She had to be as strong as her mother and do everything she could to protect Ahmed.

The Citadel, al-Darb al-Ahmar, al-Azbakeya district, Cairo

In the Citadel, Julien stood among his soldiers behind their cannons, ready and waiting for the order from Bonaparte, though feeling overwhelming sorrow and disappointment because of the grim events of the day that came out of the blow. The news arrived the day before about the revolution of the Cairenes and the killing of General Dupuy and that the al-Azhar Mosque was the centre of this revolution. He had visited al-Azhar with his friends before, admired the splendour of its Islamic architecture, spoke amicably with some sheikhs and did not feel any enmity. The anger of the Egyptians was hidden beneath the surface, but Julien did not understand any reason for it. His cannons were aimed at the neighborhoods where the revolutionaries were, adjacent to al-Azhar. Julien believed that Zainab, Badriya, and other Egyptians he knew were safe in al-Azbakeya, far away from the revolution. Other areas like Boulaq and the Old Cairo districts did not participate in the revolution. He still had high hopes that the sheikhs of al-Azhar would succeed in calming the public without further bloodshed, but he was disappointed again when the order came to fire upon the places where the rebels gathered. Julien did not think of anything but accomplishing his task and making sure that the targets were hit, but later when the order came to stop the bombardment, Julien felt relieved. The sound of enormous cannons had ceased, but he could still hear gunfire in the city. He heard that the rebels had been dispersed and that there were only a few pockets of resistance from the Moroccan fighters.

In General Caffarelli's house in al-Darb al-Ahmar neighbourhood, the young scientists were busy working when they received news of the revolution and found an al-Ja'idiya mob facing them and trying to storm the building. Some rushed to escape and seek help from the French soldiers in the Citadel. General Caffarelli was not present. The French soldiers lined up quickly and opened fire, trying to prevent the mob from storming the building, but the young scientists had never had any military training. Still, they grabbed guns and joined the defenders, the rebels were able to storm the building, and the battle took place in the corridors and rooms until the rescue arrived from the Citadel and the defenders were able to repel the attack. The rebels retreated and dispersed in every direction.

The young scholars returned to al-Azbakeya unharmed, but the attack on General Caffarelli's house was a disaster. The mob killed unarmed Frenchmen, including five of their fellow young scientists. Then the mob attacked their astronomical, scientific, and engineering instruments, breaking them into pieces and stealing some. It was a massive and irreparable loss.

Upon their return, they found calm in al-Azbakeya, in complete contrast to the horrific destruction in al-Husseiniya and al-Azhar neighbourhoods. That night they heard the details of the events of this bleak, difficult day. General Dupuy and three hundred French soldiers had been killed in the uprising, along with the five scientists who were members of the Scientific Institute. As night fell, calm prevailed, and they gathered with their friends talking:

'These Egyptians are bigoted, evil, and ignorant.'

'Traitors and hypocrites, after they pretended to be loyal to our leader.'

'Al-Azhar Sheikhs' decision to incite the mob is a betrayal of their previous agreement with Commander Bonaparte'

'Islam is a religion that has two faces: a tolerant, unbiased, and peaceful face sometimes turned towards non-Muslims, but also a hostile face that considered non-Muslims to be infidels who have no values or morals, so hatred, anger and aggressiveness appear in the eyes in place of affection and humanity.'

'Imams do not call for violence directly, but what they teach people will not produce any result except violence, extremism, and hatred of non-Muslims.'

'The ideas of freedom, justice and equality mean nothing to Egyptians. All they care about is whether what they do is following the Quran and Sharia or not; Muhammad is their ideal hero in everything.'

'Although the Turkish Caliph is of a different nationality and language, Egyptians are very loyal to him as a symbol of their loyalty to Islam; Egyptians accept humiliation and oppression from the Mamelukes and Turks because they are Muslims and resist the French reforms because we are not Muslims.'

'We should not put all the blame on Islam. There may be some extremists, but the uprising happened for practical reasons. We have introduced radical changes in the lives of these people that they are not used to and do not understand.'

The church

The young priest sat in the church with his hand holding the cross, surrounded by a few deacons and members of the congregation. The events of this tough day took them by surprise. Most Copts had barricaded themselves in their homes, and a few managed to escape outside Cairo. The atmosphere in the city was fraught with grumbling and anger, but they did not expect that the gathering of commoners around the judge's house in the morning would lead to all these grim events. The gathering became a mob which moved on and killed one of the high-ranking French officers. Then al-ja'idiya attacked the homes of Coptic Christians and other Christians in al-Jawaniya neighbourhood and looted, then burned them, and even the Muslim dwellings in this neighbourhood were not spared. They looted deposits, luggage, and shops, insulted and captured women and girls, and killed many Christians-Copts, European and Levantine. The Copts wondered commoners' mob could only be controlled by the Mameluke princes and the Turks, so would the French military and their prince Bonabarta be able to protect the Copts? They were terrified when they heard the sounds of massive explosions, shaking the earth, and saw smoke, and flames rising from al-Husseiniya and around al-Azhar. They thought that ages had passed before these huge dreadful sounds that horrified them stopped, but they could still hear the occasional gunfire and see no end to this ordeal.

Al-Sanadikya district, Cairo

Haj Mustafa's family felt safe and reassured in their large house at the beginning of the turmoil and chaos in Cairo, as it was surrounded by his loyal followers and workers. The horrific sounds of explosions were heard around them as they were trapped in their house, and no one dared to go out. Haj Mustafa did not know what happened to his friends, especially Haj Ibrahim, as his residence was right at the centre of the unrest. In the morning, a messenger from Mansour arrived to warn everyone to stay at home. Events followed quickly. Two of his friends were in Al-Azhar when the uprising began, so they hurried and took refuge in his house as it was nearby, and they all kept following the events taking place around them.

It was clear that the grumbling, complaints, and anger lurking beneath the surface for weeks had now exploded. Many sheikhs gathered in the al-Azhar Mosque and sent their readers and students to the markets to call on Muslims, saying, "Let everyone who believes in one God go to al-Azhar Mosque; this is the day of jihad, for fighting the infidels and taking revenge." People closed their shops and took up their weapons, which they had hidden away long ago, and marched towards the mosque in droves, crowding each other, led by al-Ja'idiya. They called out in their loudest voices, "God bring victory to the religion of Islam." Thousands of commoners and lower-class citizens gathered around the judge's house to complain about the injustice of the new taxes on their homes, the removal of the lane doors, and the measures taken to prevent the spread of the epidemic. They cried, "There is no God but Allah, God bring victory to the religion of Islam, God bring victory to the Sultan of the Muslims." Instead of hearing their complaints and submitting it to the Sultan, as they had hoped, the judge refused to meet them. It was the spark that ignited the flames of anger that had been lurking within for so long.

The anger soon turned into stone-throwing. The judge's house was pelted with rocks. It so happened that General Dupuy and a few French cavalrymen were caught in the events close to the judge's home and had no previous knowledge or expectation of the rage lurking beneath the surface. The mob's anger turned from the judge's house to those few Frenchmen, and they killed their Commander Dupuy with a knife. The news spread everywhere. Hidden weapons- pipes, sticks, knives, hammers, guns and gunpowder- suddenly appeared, and young men hurried to set up barricades around the alleys in anticipation of an attack by the French. Some of al Ja'idiya went around the lanes and markets, killing Christians of all denominations: Copts and those of European and Levant origin and looting and burning their homes. The Egyptians' feelings towards the French previously were different. While the French could count on both sympathisers and opponents among the Egyptian people, most were neutral. But that day everyone responded and joined the revolutionaries when they heard the call for jihad. Some of the sheikhs of al-Azhar who were cooperating with the French also joined in and contributed to igniting the fire of strife. The Egyptians behind the barricades successfully repelled the French infantry attacks and continued to resist throughout the night.

The French were surprised, and Bonaparte was quick to contact the sheikhs of al-Azhar to try to contain the events, but he found nothing other than procrastination from them. The next day he gave orders to bombard the city, and bombs rained down from the citadel towards al-Husseiniya, al-Ghourayya, al-Fahameen and al-Azhar. After hours of successive massive explosions and horrific destruction in the neighbourhoods, the sheikhs of al-Azhar rushed to meet

Bonaparte pleading to stop the bombardment, he agreed after his cannons had extinguished the fire of the uprising. Some Moroccans continued to fire until they ran out of ammunition, but they were the last. Night fell, everyone dispersed, and only devastation, destruction, the groans of the wounded, and the bodies of the dead remained. The conversation took place in the house of Haj Mustafa:

> 'The list of taxes on property and real estate that they attached to the junctions, roads and markets today was the spark that ignited the anger of the mob. Al-Ja'idiya were waiting for a reason to rise against the French, and many the sheikhs of al-Azhar agreed with them without considering the consequences.'
>
> 'The sheikhs of al-Azhar should have been the first to know that the knives and sticks of the lower classes and al-Ja'idiya could not be a match to Bonabarta's cannons.'
>
> 'Let us affix no blame on them; we have waited long enough for the Sultan's army.'

Mansour was absent from the scene because the French summoned him quickly and told him to find out the names of the sheikhs who incited the revolution. He knew a lot about the instigators, and he knew that the French had many eyes in the streets, so he must report everything he knew correctly to continue to be trusted by them. His friend Sheikh Abdul Ghani was one of these instigators and Mansour did not want to cause him harm, yet he had to report him among the others.

It happened in December 1798

Al Azbakeya district, Cairo

The events of October led to a change in the French view of the Egyptians; the warm and friendly approach cooled and turned to discord, and they became wary of Muslims, so the French evacuated the population around the al-Azbakeya pond and brought the French to live in it so that they would all be in one place that is easy to defend. The French also refrained from walking in the streets unarmed. Egyptians felt this new sense of disharmony, which made them feel insecure. Most people stopped walking in the streets or markets from sunset to daybreak. Eventually, the French took control of the situation again. Weeks passed, and the monotony of normal life returned to what it was before the uprising.

The young French friends continued to appear at the dining house run by Zainab, now alone after Badriya's loss. They noticed that Zainab no longer sang in the evenings. Julien was always thinking about Zainab, and he repeatedly tried to talk to her, but she always appeared busy with work, and the conversation each time was no more than a short dialogue for a few minutes. He gave a generous tip to a waiter to tell him more about Zainab. He knew that she was unmarried, and she was looking after a paralysed brother and refused all marriage proposals. He knew what happened to her at the time of rebellion and regretted the death of the nice and lively Badriya. He felt very sorry when he heard what happened to Zainab during the bombardment of al-Husseiniya and al-Azhar. He realised that hundreds of peaceful Cairenes were killed through no fault of their own, but it just happened that they were within range of the French cannons at the time of the revolution.

Julien asked Zainab for a chat when she was not busy at work, but she smiled at him and gently apologised that she was busy all the time. Her smile charmed him, but he was puzzled and disappointed by her response to his invitation.

Julien and his friends also met again in the palace garden overlooking the al-Azbakeya pond, talking about their life in

Cairo, and what was happening there. They talked about a letter sent from the Levant by Bakir Pasha and Ibrahim Bey to the people of Egypt attacking the French for their disbelief and denial of religions and reiterating to the Egyptians that the French came to eliminate Islam. The letter called them to jihad for the sake of Islam. Then the friends mentioned that their leader Bonaparte had told the sheikhs to write and distribute to the country a leaflet to deny what Ibrahim Bey said, so they did so, but the people were troubled because of rumours about a decree received from His Majesty the Sultan, so the Sheikhs issued another leaflet exonerating the French from what was said against them in this rumoured decree and urging people to obey the French and to pay the Kharaj taxes to them. The friends' conversation continued:

> 'Throughout the ages, religion has always been used in the struggle for power and influence. The Mamelukes commit obscenities forbidden by Islam, such as sexual immoralities, the sexual abuse of children, drinking alcohol, looting, theft and corruption. Yet, they appear in front of the Egyptians whom they robbed and enslaved, as if they were the protectors of Islam, calling people to

jihad and throwing Egyptians to their death so that they can return to their luxurious palaces.'

'Humans invented religion because they needed religion, and then religion became the main source of hatred and violence between humans.'

'Only religion gives people comfort and peace, and it is the one that explains to them all the mysteries of the universe that are impossible for them to comprehend. It is the one that gives meaning to their lives and solves the problem of the fear of death. It is a solace in times of sadness and provides tranquillity in times of fear. The hope for another life reduces the instinctive fear of death, so people defend religion with their lives. People can't give up religion unless they find an alternative that can give them peace with themselves and give meaning to their lives. This is what happened in France. People saw an alternative, and in future, this may happen in many countries of the world.'

'But as in France and despite the revolution, Catholicism still exists strongly, and religion will remain until the end of the world because no alternative can give people what it gives.'

'Don't blame the Egyptians for their religiosity. Look at Julien; despite his enthusiasm for the revolution, he did not abandon his Catholicism and will not abandon it, no matter how strong the argument may be.'

'Europeans also used religion to justify attacking Muslims during the Crusades.'

'But the Crusades are history that has passed, and passed forever those days in which the Europeans fought in the name of Christianity, unlike these Egyptians, who fought for no reason other than to support religion. Different Muslim invaders have controlled Egypt one after the other for hundreds of years. Despite the injustice and oppression inflicted on the Egyptians, the invaders pretended to be the protectors of Islam, and so the Egyptians did not fight them.'

In his new home in al-Azbakeya, Ahmed fell asleep and seemed satisfied and happy, while Zainab kept thinking about the horrors she saw during the Cairo uprising. Badriya had died, and Zainab was alone to face life. She had already lost her mother, and so was without a parent's tenderness, care and guidance. The hostility and aggressiveness of her neighbours in al-Husseiniya had increased since she started singing to a French audience in her restaurant. She no longer felt safe in her old home, so she bought another house in al-Azbakeya that was close to the restaurant. Her new home was also close to where the French lived, which gave her a greater sense of security, so she hid what was left of the gold dinars in it as well.

The bonds of friendship between her and her new neighbours grew, and she no longer felt that she was an outcast. On the contrary, she felt nothing but affection and kindness from them. She paid off all her debt, as she earned a lot from her trade and the running of the restaurant. She had to stop singing, which she loved because she was always busy working. Immersion in work was taking her away from the sadness buried deep down.

Her heart bled as she watched Ahmed's disease progress, knowing that she could do nothing to help. She was able to present her brother to a French doctor, and he told her that he could not cure him. Ahmed's disease affected the muscles of the whole body and no one knew either a cause or a treatment. He also hinted that Ahmed was in the last stages of the disease and that he would not live long. Zainab knew this deep inside already just from observing her brother and seeing the continuous deterioration in his condition; however, the French doctor's words broke her heart because he eliminated the last glimmers of hope she had. Ahmed could no longer move his arms or legs and was completely dependent on having Ali and his wife by his side to care for his needs. Zainab's heart broke as she watched how intelligent, brilliant, polite and courteous her brother was. He never complained to anyone about the merciless and cruel disease. Even as his condition worsened over time, still kept smiling. He was strong-willed, a strength he inherited from his mother. Zainab felt that she had not inherited as much strength as life's adversities frequently overcame her.

Ahmed had become a student at al-Azhar after studying at the Kotaab. Because of his intelligence, he not only studied Islamic jurisprudence and Arabic grammar as others do, but also studied astronomy, engineering and mathematics, taught by one of the disciples of the great Sheikh Hassan al-Jabarti. But the dreaded disease forced him to leave his beloved studies behind when it reached the point where he could no longer move his hands.

What Ahmed heard about the scientific advances of the French and their superiority in knowledge caught his imagination. So, Zainab took him to the reading library recently established by the French in the house of Hassan Kashif Jarkas in the neighbourhood of al-Nasiriyah. How proud she was of him when she saw him talking to the Frenchmen about astronomical observations and mathematics in the way of those who knew these things. She was so much delighted when she saw that the Frenchmen were truly interested in talking to him, as they brought him some of their strange astronomical and geometric instruments, and he seemed to understand and admire them very much. Her sadness was profound that the progress of his relentless disease had prevented him from continuing to pursue his interest in science.

Zainab lay in bed, exhausted, tired from the day's hard work, not far from her brother, but still thinking about her restaurant. She hadn't seen anything from the French other than affection, kindness and honesty, and she greatly regretted the feeling of hatred that Egyptians had towards the French and their strong desire to get rid of them. It was not difficult for her to notice Julien's interest in her and his repeated attempts to get close to her; many did the same, and she did not pay attention to them, but she did not know why she felt that Julien was different from the others, though perhaps the fact his interest in her was so obvious it satisfied her pride.

Al-Sanadikya district, Cairo

After the immense destruction of the neighbourhoods by Bonaparte's bombs in October, the peace and serenity of the evening get-together in the house of Haj Mustafa had vanished. They saw hundreds of dead neighbours, friends and workers and many of their homes were destroyed, and even this elite bunch of wealthy men were not spared from harm. Naaman al-Roomy, the Greek Christian and his family escaped harm because his house was in al-Muski, away from the events. Still, al-ja'idiya mob invaded the home of Saad Allah, the Coptic, and looted his belongings and goods. Fortunately, he and his family escaped a certain death by leaving just before the mob attacked. French cannons destroyed a large part of Haj Ibrahim's house, and he was also lucky to have been able to find shelter for himself and his family during the bombardment. Sheikh Abdul Ghani was mistreated and badly beaten after being arrested on charges of incitement, and a fine of one-thousand Riyal Fransah was imposed on him. Friends hurried to collect the money, and he was eventually released after he was close to death. Sheikh Ismail was spared because he did not agree to stir up the commoners and did not participate in the uprising. However, the French arrested six of the senior ulema who proved to be the heads of sedition and imprisoned them. Then they took them up to the Citadel, shot them, and threw their bodies from the high wall in the back of the Citadel. The French had appointed a roomy, a Christian man of Greek origin, named Barttalmin as head of police and deputy governor. He roamed the neighbourhoods with his soldiers, searching for loot and weapons. He arrested many, imposed imprisonment, beating, and punishment, slaughtered many who had participated in the uprising and threw their bodies in the Nile. The violence and destruction continued until the French established full control again. When the unrest settled and security was restored, the friends returned to their business, trade and workshops, and the evening gatherings resumed, but without the joy, fun, and humour as before. Resentment and regret prevailed.

Mansour remained among them, but no one knew he was working in secret with the French, or that it was he who informed on Sheikh Abdul Ghani. All the friends knew was that Mansour went with Sheikh Ismail and some other sheikhs and notable merchants to intercede on behalf of Sheikh Abdul Ghani with Sari Askar the Great, asking for more time to pay the fine imposed on him. Mansour heard Sheikh Abdul Ghani screaming and crying out for him while he was being beaten, hoping that Mansour's influence with the French might ease his treatment. For a moment, Mansour felt a lump in his throat and felt pity for his friend, but he quickly swallowed it. He did not regret snitching on him as he always justified the harm he inflicted on others by telling himself that he too had suffered a lot of pain and injustice in his life and that he could not take any more, and that he had to protect and secure himself at all costs. There was no protection better than loyalty to the military; it did not matter if they were the military of the Turks or the military of the French. Mansour put his thoughts aside and joined the conversation with his friends with the rumbling of the hookah and the sound of sipping from coffee cups in the background:

'How did Bonabarta allow his soldiers to enter al-Azhar Mosque and desecrate its sanctity? They entered while riding the horses and tied their horses to its Qibla, and they broke and looted everything, threw the Qur'an on the ground, and trampled it with their shoes, and insulted and beat everyone they found.'

'The Francees respected al-Azhar more than anywhere else in Cairo, and they did not pass through this area except rarely and made it the safest place in Cairo. Still, the sheikhs incited the public and made al-Azhar the centre of the mutiny without appreciating the consequences. Then the mob killed Dupuy and many of their knights and soldiers; the Francees considered this a betrayal of their agreement. In any case, the sheikhs had gone to Bonabarta and now he ordered his soldiers to evacuate al-Azhar Mosque. Peace and tranquilly prevailed again, and al-Azhar has regained its status and prestige.'

'Al-Azhar will not regain its status and respect unless these infidels leave the land of Muslims.'

'Bonabarta plans to stay, so he started to fortify the entrances to the Egyptian land, Alexandria, Rashid and Damietta. He fortified them to make them impregnable and constructed fortifications in Cairo and its suburbs that prevent another uprising.'

'They created a battalion of the Moroccans of al-Fahameen, gave them weapons and war machines, trained them, granted them military ranks, and sent them to Lower Egypt to suppress sedition against the Francees. They taught them on how to fight in their way, their laws, and the meaning of their signals. They are trained just like that of the French Army.'

'We have no resources to fight them; salvation will only come with the arrival of the Sultan's army.'

'Al-Arwam and al-Shwam Christians, whose homes were looted in the Jawaniya neighbourhood, complained to Bonabarta about the devastation inflicted on them and claimed that the Muslims attacked them only because they were associated with the Francees. However, al-Ja'idiya and other riffraff who looted their homes also looted the homes of Muslims that were adjacent to them and robbed them of their belongings as well. Those who have incited these villains are playing with fire.'

'Barttalmin was able to return some of the goods looted from the Christians. The French soldiers were able to arrest some Arab Bedouins and recover what they had looted from the pilgrims upon their return from the pilgrimage as well. They caught them, tied them up with ropes, and brought them into Cairo. They were paraded down the streets with drummers in the lead, followed by the looted loads and camels for all the Cairenes to see.'

'That's because Bonabarta never allows looting. When some French soldiers went to Suez ahead of him, the people of Suez fled, and the French soldiers took what they found in the town of coffee, belongings and goods. So when Bonabarta came, the merchants spoke to him and complained about the loss of their goods and properties, and he recovered from the military what they took and promised the merchants that he would recover the rest or pay for it in Cairo. He asked them to write a list of the looted items.'

'They arranged the Diwan on a new system after it had been stopped because of the uprising, and they established many new buildings, castles, roads, bridges and mills. They did not use forced labour; they gave the men more than their usual wages and fewer working hours. The Francees love work and fairness.'

'Their love for justice does not show in the issue of hanging lanterns in front of houses at night; they imposed a fine if the lantern's flame was extinguished or its oil ran out. As if people had no job except lanterns and looking after lanterns, especially on the long winter nights!'

'They paved the hill next to The Lemon Arch, and made a mill that can turn from the force of the wind at the top, and made another similar mill at al-Rawda. These amazing mills can grind huge amounts of wheat with the least effort and time. They also built a massive hospital in al-Rawda and established mills and hospitals in Alexandria, Rosetta and Damietta.'

'This wondrous printing press, which they brought from their country, prints large numbers of letters, statements and publications very quickly and with little effort.'

'The large French balloon, which was intended to impress the Egyptians, failed to do so; although they had brought a specialist in balloons from

Fransah, it traveled a short distance in the air and then fell. It was not what they said it was a vehicle that could travel to distant countries carrying news and correspondence, so it turned out to be like a kite that people use for fun in seasons and weddings.'

'This caused them great embarrassment in public, but Fransah is an advanced country in civilisation and the Francees love science. The houses of the fleeing mameluke princes in the Nasiriyah neighbourhood were dedicated to establishing a library and places to meet engineers, doctors, pharmacists, chemists, blacksmiths, precision machine makers, and more. Some of the ulema of al-Azhar intend to go to watch, and I will go with them. There are many things in science we have no experience with; some ulema refused to go because they do not want to show that they agree with the Francees.'

Nasiriyah Lane, al-Darb al-Gadeed, Cairo

Haj Mustafa and Sheikh Ismail went with several merchants and ulema to visit the Egyptian Scientific Institute and other scientific buildings; as they had heard much about them. The French had demolished several houses belonging to Mameluke princes and took the finest stones and marble as material for their buildings. Within them, they allocated a place for scientists and craftsmen of all kinds: astronomers, people of knowledge, mathematicians, engravers, artists, and many others. Everyone gazed with wonder at the library, which contained an extensive collection of French books they kept and prepared to be available to their students and to those who wanted to review them. If a Muslim came to see them, they would not prevent him from entering their dearest places and would receive him with friendliness and a show of pleasure, especially if they saw in him the ability or knowledge or aspiration to look at these books and learn from them. Then they would show them to him politely, presenting books that had been printed containing regions of the world, knowledge of animals, birds, the history of the ancients and other nations, and the stories of the prophets with their pictures, bodies and miracles, which baffled the Egyptians mind.

The Egyptians gazed in awe at images of other countries, coasts, seas, pyramids, hills of Upper Egypt, ancient temples, painted shapes and movies, animal races, birds, plants, herbs, medical sciences, anatomy, engineering machines, weight pulling, and many Islamic books translated into French. They also had many dictionaries of other languages that allowed them to translate material into French, or vice versa, with ease.

The visitors also saw strange astronomical instruments that were well made, wonderful machines with strange compositions, tubes used to look at the stars and planets and observe their magnitudes and shapes, and expensive clocks that recorded even the seconds; Their artists could draw pictures of human beings in such a realistic manner that the viewer would think they were real.

The French also assigned workspaces for engineers, the manufacture of fine tiny machines, doctors' residences, medical tools and machines with bottles and fluids needed for making medicines, and strange distillation machines. They allocated a place for carpenters, machinery makers, timber, windmills, wagons that were needed for them in their works, engineering and craftsmen, and another place for blacksmiths with anvils and huge iron lathes for the manufacture of machines, and at the top of these places makers of precision things, watches, elaborate engineering machines. Nothing like any of it existed in Egypt.

The Egyptians did not have time to see everything because walking through all the buildings and workshops would take weeks. The most amazing thing was how the French had accomplished all of these achievements in the short time they had been in Egypt. Some visitors expressed a desire to return to this place again, and they were made to feel very welcome.

Al-Husseiniya district, Cairo

Although many students and scholars from al-Azhar and many followers of Sheikh Abd al-Rahman were killed during the various events of the revolution, the number of young people attending the sheikh's lessons with Hussein after Isha prayer in the mosque has increased. The killing of six of al-Azhar's faithful and respected sheikhs in the citadel sparked outrage, as they were among the valued leading scholars who taught people about religion, served the community, and interceded for anyone who was in distress. Sheikh Abd al-Rahman began his speech:

> 'God Almighty says in his Holy Book, "and do not say those who are killed for the sake of Allah are dead but alive, but you do not feel," and he also says, "and do not count those who were killed for

the sake of Allah as dead but alive with their Lord they will live." This is the truth of the great God. Do not say, O believers, that those mujahideen who were killed for the sake of Allah are dead, but they are alive with an extraordinary life of their own in their graves, the way of which only Allah knows. Do not think that those who were killed for the sake of Allah are dead and feel nothing. They are alive and have a feeling of life in the vicinity of their Lord, for whom they fought and died for Him. Their livelihood is in Paradise, and they are blessed.'

Sheikh Abd al-Rahman knew that al-Azhar sheikhs wrote leaflets at the request of Bonaparte, which they signed as if they were their own and distributed all over the country. In them, they rebutted a letter that had previously been written by Bakir Pasha and Ibrahim Bey to the people of Egypt. In the sheikhs' leaflet, they urged the Egyptians to obey the French and to pay al-Kharaj (taxes) to them, this had caused confusion and concern among the people, so sheikh Abd al-Rahman went on to say as everyone nodded in agreement:

'The end of the time of the infidels on the land of Egypt is near; the letter has arrived from Ibrahim

Bey exposing the intentions of the infidel Francees and calling for jihad. When the Sultan's army comes, the Mameluke princes and mujahideen will join forces to defend our honour and religion, so prepare yourselves with all you can, prepare for this coming day. These infidel Franks are hypocrites and deceitful people, and their chief, Bonabarta has made the sheikhs and religious scholars go along with his wicked plans and repeat his lies. I say to these al-Azhar sheikhs, are you Muslims, or are you infidels? And I say to you, wait for the day of jihad. The day of jihad is near, and we will all rise united as one, to uphold righteousness and religion. Whoever takes a religion other than Islam is an infidel, and the leadership of our people cannot be given to a disbeliever. The greatest sedition is coexistence according to the law of human beings without the law of God, and the tyrant Bonabarta rules without what God has revealed. He will suffer a miserable fate and torment in the hereafter. We do not prostrate ourselves to anyone other than God, and we only listen to the Messenger of God.'

'The soldiers of the tyrant Bonabarta entered the al-Azhar Mosque riding their horses and scattered inside its corridors, halls, and rooms and tied their horses to the Qibla. They broke its lanterns and smashed the cubicles of the students and attendees, tore books to pieces, and looted whatever they found of the belongings and utensils and the bowls and what was kept in the cupboards and cabinets. They threw the books and Qurans on the ground and tread on them with their shoes.'

'Unveiled women walk shamelessly in the streets, and servants and slaves prepare the way for them as if they were princesses. Brothels and bars operate publicly for everyone to see in al-Azbakeya and are no longer a secret. They have even remade a building next to al-Azbakeya in the form of French buildings, where women and men meet for fun and decadence.'

'Bonabarta released the hands of Barttalmin, the Christian, to kill Muslims, and allowed the Christians to wear large turbans and luxury clothes and ride mules and carry weapons like Muslims. Christians now show malice to Muslims, and

Bonabarta seeks to insult and mock Muslims by equating them with Christians.'

'He is an infidel man who leads an army of infidels. His capture of Egypt encourages Christians to humiliate Muslims.'

Sheikh Abd al-Rahman brought the discussion to a conclusion:

'God loves those who are patient in distress and blesses them with quick relief. Wait for the day of jihad and strive for the sake of God with your money and your souls and let them taste the torment in this world before the torment of the hereafter.'

The church

After Sunday mass, people talked about the devastation, destruction and killing that befell Christians during the uprising. The French were able to control Cairo only with difficulty, and could only return a small portion of the Christian's looted belongings to their owners. Hence, some reassurance returned to their hearts, and people said:

'Bonabarta sacrificed the Copts to support Islam and could not protect us from the attacks of al-Ja'idiya or from the ensuing theft, looting, killing and humiliation.'

'I can't entirely agree with that. Al-Ja'idiya bastards are not afraid of Bonabarta because they don't think about the consequences, and they have nothing to lose. But those junior sheikhs of al-Azhar who incite them want to take revenge on the Christians every time any Muslims suffer. We were safe in the days of the Turks and the Mamelukes, we are now caught between the hammer of al-Ja'idiya and the anvil of the French.'

'Bonabarta appointed Mu'allim Gerges al-Gohary as the general public director, giving him authority over all other directors. Still, he was keen to have a Frenchman with him to monitor him.'

'Bonabarta only takes care of the Copts like Mu'allim Gerges al-Gohary because they are the sole people who can handle the country's administration and finances, which are essential to Bonabarta. Still, he intends to introduce a new tax system that would allow him to dispense with the services of the Copts, who have been doing this work alone for hundreds of years.'

'Bonabarta wants to show his inclination towards Islam in front of Muslims. Still, he is imbued with the spirit of equality and fraternity, so he will protect the different faiths, whether Jews or Christians. He wrote a letter to Mu'allim Gerges al-Gohary in which he said: "that it is a pleasure to protect Copts, who will no longer be the object of contempt and when circumstances allow, a thing that I do not see far away, I may allow Copts to observe their religious rites in public, as is the case in Europe, where everyone is free to follow their faith." He added, "I will severely punish the villages where Copts were killed during the revolutions that broke out, while you can from now on tell the members of your sect that I allow them to carry weapons, ride mules and horses, put turbans on their heads, and decorate themselves and their dwellings with what they want."'

'But this was not the case with the Christians from the Levant, as they went back to wearing small black and blue turbans and stopped wearing white turbans and coloured Kashmiri cloths because the Francees prevented them from doing so.'

'Bonabarta did that as a punishment to them because they deceived him by claiming that the Muslims were conspiring to start a new revolution. They said it for their own purposes. When Bonabarta investigated, it was proved that this claim was untrue.'

'Perhaps he did not deliberately harm the Christians, but he did not show them any evidence of his compassion as he did with Muslims. He endeavoured with his words and deeds to win the hearts of the Muslims.'

'The Patriarch said that the Copts would not welcome the Francees unless they were free from all religious motives and did not intend to interfere with our Orthodox faith. The French did not show any desire to interfere in people's beliefs, unlike al-Arwam, the Greeks, and the Franks, the Europeans, who settled in al-Muski, who have long criticised our true faith.'

A letter written by Bakir Pasha and Ibrahim Bey to the people of Egypt was sent to Mustafa Bey, who could not help but deliver it to Bonaparte out of his fear of the French. The letter was translated for Bonaparte and it said after the initiation:

"The French, may god exterminate them and may their flags be covered with shame because they are infidels and a recalcitrant people who do not believe in the message of the Prophet, peace be upon him, and mock all religions and deny the resurrection and what God has prepared in it of reward and punishment. They believe that blind chance is the dominion over life and death and that the soul is material, and that the bodies, after their dissolution in the earth, do not return to life again and are not followed by account or judgment. Based on this belief they have put their hands on their temples and expelled their priests and monks. To them, the revealed books are nothing but myths and fabricated lies, the Qur'an, the Torah and the Gospel are myths, Moses, Jesus, and Muhammad are ordinary men, and all men have been created alike and nothing distinguishes them from each other, and that each of them has the right to believe what comes to him, and on these beliefs, they have built all their

deeds and laid down diabolic laws. These actions have shaken Europe, which has shed abundant blood as a result. You know what the honourable religion of Islam commands you to do, so you should pay attention to what they spread among you because their purpose is to destroy Mecca, Medina and Jerusalem, slaughter all the people in them except the children, and divide their inheritance and lands. Those who remain alive will be forced to follow their principles and learn their language, and Islam will disappear from the Earth. Understand what the result will be if every Muslim does not carry Islam in their heart and fight against these useless men. Pay attention to the traps that have been set for you. The lion does not care about foxes, whether they are many or few."

The sheikhs of al-Azhar wrote these leaflets at the request of Bonaparte, signed them, printed them in the printing press brought by the campaign, and distributed copies all across the country. It read:

"We seek refuge in Allah from temptation, both those that are apparent and those that are hidden, and we strive to disavow ourselves in the eyes of Allah from those who seek

pay al-Kharaj taxes that you have to pay. The faith is the advice. Peace be on you."

A signed publication was sent by all ulema of Egypt, refuting the claims made against the French of what was stated against them in that decree that was supposedly sent by His Majesty the Sultan. The publication read:

"Advice from ulema of Islam in Egypt. We tell you, O believers, people of the cities and provinces, and rural inhabitants of Arabs and peasants, that Ibrahim Bey, Murad Bey and the rest of the Mameluke state sent several correspondences and communications to the rest of the Egyptian provinces to stir up strife between people, and claimed by lying and smearing that they were from Hadrat (an honorific Arab title) his Majesty the Sultan and some of his ministers. The reason for this was that they got severe torment, agony and anguish and became severely angry at the ulema of Egypt and its subjects because they did not agree to flee with them and to leave their families and homeland; they wanted to create strife and evil between the community and the French military for the destruction of the country and the destruction of the entire parish, and that the

severity of what happened to them from the excess anguish by the destruction of their state and depriving them of the protected Kingdom of Egypt. If these papers were truly from Hadrat Sultan, he would have sent them openly through his certain deputies. We tell you that the French sect, in particular out of the rest of the Frankish sects, always love Muslims and their religion and hate the infidels and their nature, and they are friends of his majesty the Sultan. They support him and are attached to him for his affection, his charities and his help, they love those who support him and hate those who are hostile to him. Therefore, the French and Mosco (Russia) are very hostile to each other, and for this reason, the French help Hadrat Sultan to fight the people of the Mosco country, and God willing, he will defeat them. We advise you, O people of the Egyptian provinces, not to stir up strife or evils among the community and not to oppose the French soldiers with any kind of harm which would bring damage, destruction and affliction to you. And do not listen to the words of the corruptors and do not obey the command of the wasteful who corrupt the earth and who do not reform; otherwise, you will become sorry for what you have done. You must pay al-Kharaj taxes required of you to all those who are commissioned to collect it to be safe and secure in your homelands and ensure the security of your families and money, because Hadrat Sari Askar the Great, and Prince of the Armies Bonabarta, agreed with us that he does not dispute anyone in the religion of Islam and does not oppose us in what God has prescribed of rulings and lifts all other grievances from the parish. The taxes that he levied are limited and his aim is to remove the influence of the previous tyrants. Do not pin your hopes on Ibraham and Murad and instead return your loyalty to your master, the owner of the kingdoms and the creator of all people. His Prophet and His Holy Messenger said: "Conflict is asleep; may Allah curse whoever awakens it among the nations." On him be the best prayer and peace. The greeting is the end."

It happened in January 1799

Al-Azbakeya district, Cairo

Bonaparte sat in his office in the Grand al-Azbakeya Palace, examining some papers, maps and books, waiting for dinner. His beautiful companion Pauline Fourés, whom some liked to call, Cleopatra, was busy preparing the banquet and would join him in welcoming his guests. Pauline brought joy and fun back to his life after the gloom that overwhelmed him when he became sure of his wife Josephine's infidelity. He first saw Pauline when he opened al-Azbakeya Garden, a young beautiful blonde lass with a round face. It was not easy to approach her; Napoleon knew that she was Lieutenant Fourés' wife, so he sent him on a mission to Paris to get him out of the way so that he could approach Pauline. At sea, Lieutenant Fourés fell into the hands of the British, who sent him back to Egypt to find his wife with Napoleon. They soon divorced, and the beautiful Pauline became the companion of Commander Bonaparte.

Many events followed the uprising of the commoners and lower classes in Cairo that took him by surprise. He was not the kind of person who could tolerate mutiny or insurrection. It was not easy to suppress a revolution in a city of 600,000 people which was the same size as Paris. He did not want to use excessive force, but he could not find an alternative, so he issued the order, and the cannons fired from the citadel to knock down the neighbourhoods of Cairo. The revolt was put down, and calm returned to Cairo, but he deeply mourned the death of General Dupuy and his close friend and aide Sulkowski in this revolt.

The time had come for him to turn his attention to the danger arising from the Levant. He received news on 20 October that the Sultan's armies were gathering in Syria to attack Egypt by land at a time when he was expecting another attack by the Sultan's forces from the sea. He determined that the only course of action was to destroy the Sultan's army in the Levant before having to face the naval expedition as well. Time was not on his side, and he would have to move quickly. General Desaix's campaign had finally succeeded as he was in control of all of Upper Egypt. Desaix had defeated Murad Bey and captured his Nile fleet, so now with the whole Egyptian countryside under his full control, it was time for the Levant campaign. He planned to incite Syrian and Lebanese Christians, Jews, and the Druze to revolt against the Sultan and ally with him. The destruction of the Sultan's army in Syria would allow him to take control of Haifa, Jaffa and Acre and deprive the English fleet of the use of these ports. He could then set out for Constantinople and from there march to India to fulfil his dreams of an Eastern empire just like that of Alexander the Great. Ahmed al-Gezzar Pasha, whose name meant "the butcher" was all that stood between him and the fulfilment of his dreams. They did not call him the butcher for no reason, however. He had earned this well-deserved nickname by killing seven of his wives, and his servants and associates knew that the punishment for any negligence or delay in carrying out his orders was the amputation of an ear, nose or eye. The cruelty he showed his enemies, and the brutal manner he used to treat Christians had to be expected. He was also unprincipled and opportunistic. He had been an enemy of the Mamelukes and Turks, but when the French arrived, he reached a peace agreement with the Sultan and helped Ibrahim Bey after he fled Egypt. Bonaparte tried to entice him to ally with him instead, but al-Gezzar refused to even meet his messenger. Once peace with the Mamelukes and the Sultan was established, al-Gezzar seized all of Palestine, occupied Gaza and al-Arish, and announced that he would liberate Egypt from the French. Crossing the desert is impossible in the summer months, so Napoleon needed to move immediately to accomplish his mission and return before then.

With the return of General Desaix from upper Egypt, news arrived from Bonaparte's friend Vivant Denon and the scientists who accompanied the campaign as well. They described the wonders they saw in Luxor, Esna, Edfu, Philae, and Dendera and of magnificent and very well-constructed temples, buildings, and statues, whose beauty was beyond description and even surpassed those of the ancient Greeks. Denon said the Egyptians appeared as giants. Napoleon wondered at the contradiction between ancient Egyptian civilisation's greatness and contemporary Egyptians' backwardness. Napoleon was impressed by the weather in Egypt, the agriculture and the fertility of the land in the Nile Valley, but he saw the modern Egyptians as a dull, despondent and stupid people in need of science and civilisation. These contemporary Egyptians were dazzled by the buttons on the uniforms of French soldiers, and would give nearly anything in exchange for just one of them. They did not even know how to make anything as simple as a wheelbarrow or air and water mills. In the Egyptian villages, they had never seen as simple a tool as a pair of scissors.

In her new home in al-Azbakeya, Zainab was sitting and talking to her brother Ahmed. She was smiling and talking with humour to hide the pain and despair inside her, as she needed solace for her sad heart. She knew a place that might give her peace and renew hope. She kissed Ahmed and left.

Ahmed was left alone with his thoughts. Over the years, he learned how to live with adversity, face life's harshness, and cope with his ruthless disease. He realised a long time ago that there was no reprieve from this dreaded paralysis. His muscles were getting weaker and weaker as time went by. This started with his inability to move his legs, and then the disease spread relentlessly though his body, until he was now unable to move any part of his body except his face. His breathing became heavy and slow; he now felt close to death. This was unquestionable. There was no point in feeling sorry for himself, which would just make him miserable without gaining anything in return. What he had always done and must do now was to find peace with himself and live with what was available to him. It was not always the case that health and physical strength gave peace of mind. Many people he had seen with money, power and health were unhappy inside. Contentment with what was available to him gave him peace and serenity. He enjoyed many of the pleasures of life when he could move, and even after he was paralysed, with help from Ali he was able to visit his friends, go for a picnic with them on the Nile shore and go to the al-Kotaab and the mosque. His donkey and dog added much joy to his life. His dog had aged and become weak; maybe he was on the way to the end, like himself. There were still many sources of joy in his life, and he was content with that. Seeing the beautiful and full of fun Zainab next to him gave him the most joy and delight; he still met a number of his friends and felt pleasure in talking to them. Ali and his wife did everything for him, even putting in front of him the Qur'an and other books he liked to read and turning their pages for him. He found in this healing for his soul.

Al-Husseiniya district, Cairo

After a day of hard work in his workshop, Hussein rushed to join his peers in prayer and to hear Sheikh Abd al-Rahman's lesson in Islamic jurisprudence that followed the prayer. The presence of the Franks in Egypt brought much work to the blacksmithing workshops owned by his father. In the beginning, the work came from the Mameluke princes who prepared to fight the Franks. They took everything they needed without paying for it. After the French settled in Cairo, they began a lot of building and construction, which caused prosperity to his industry as the French were paying the full cost and didn't argue or haggle about prices. The French still sent orders to his workshop, even though they had those great iron lathes and other machinery they brought to make with great precision whatever they needed. Hussein saw the gentleness of the French towards the Egyptians and the demonstration of their knowledge as nothing but despicable tricks to deceive people, in order to first dominate them and then take them away from the religion of righteousness, but Hussein was not deceived by that, he could see for himself the decadence, immorality and lewdness which was the nature of the French.

Sheikh Abd al-Rahman advised him to marry Suoad, the daughter of a wealthy merchant, and his parents welcomed this, so he married her and brought her to live with them in the big house in al-Husseiniya. Suoad was a good girl. She was overweight like many wealthy ladies and girls, but she was a virtuous Muslim who prayed the prayers on time and repeated supplications and entreaties. She was always submissive to him and rushed to please him. He tried to forget Zainab, but he couldn't. The thought of her beautiful face and sweet memories of their childhood together tormented his heart. He couldn't share these feelings with anyone else, and so kept them buried deep inside. He arrived at the mosque in time for prayer and listened to the lesson on jurisprudence afterwards. Sheikh Abd al-Rahman was adept at explaining the judicial rulings, searching for their truths and references, and presenting the beliefs of the true faith. The conversation took place after the lesson:

> 'The Francees military and their chief Desaix had returned from Upper Egypt. Yacoub, the Coptic, was with them, who knew the area and showed them the hiding places of the Mamelukes. They let Yacoub the Coptic do with the Muslims whatever he wanted on their behalf.'
>
> 'They raised the status of the Copts, other Christians living in the country, and the Jews. Hence, these Christians rode horses, holding swords just like Muslims because they served the French, walking proudly, saying obscenities and

boasting of their humiliation of the Muslims. There is no power but from God the Almighty.'

'The Franks' invasion is a punishment from God for abandoning Sharia law and the true religion.'

Sheikh Abd al-Rahman ended the meeting by saying that 'the infidel Franks were aiming to eliminate Islam.' Still, he said, 'the Turks and Mamelukes belong to our faith and are fighting to defend our religion, as is the army of the Sultan, the Caliph of the Muslims in the Levant and with him, the Mameluke princes. Bonabarta, the hypocrite liar is going to the Levant with an army of infidels. This will be his annihilation and the annihilation of the army of the infidels, God willing, so let's be prepared and ready to eliminate what is left of them as soon as Sultan's army reaches us.'

The church

Some of the Church congregation met when Father Athanasius was not present. Three youths close to Mu'allim Yacoub, along with many other young people, called for this meeting. They discussed how Mu'allim Yacoub returned victorious with General Desaix from the Upper Egypt campaign. Mu'allim Yacoub showed heroism when he defeated the Mamelukes in the battle of Ain Qusiya near Assiut, raising his status in the eyes of the French, and he learned their language and learned their methods of war and war planning. He also learned about the great civilisation that existed in France and about its science, culture and style of governance, and he even learned a lot from the French about the history of Egypt. The country was not always just a province affiliated with occupiers. In the past, Egypt was an independent country and had a great civilisation of its own. The current civilisation of the Turks or the French was taken from the ancient Egyptians, but the occupiers and the Ottomans had abolished Egyptian nationalism, and Egypt became just a province belonging to foreign powers. Now was the time for Egypt to become independent once again and restore its ancient civilisation. Mu'allim Yacoub said: "we must get rid of the Ottomans and Mamelukes who enslaved us and plundered our wealth for hundreds of years. We saw nothing but chaos, violence and extravagance under the Ottoman Mameluke rule. We can only get rid of the Ottomans and Mamelukes by allying with a powerful country like Fransah, and we can gain independence from the Sultan only if we ally with the Francees. All Egyptians, Copts, Jews and Muslims must join forces to help the Francees expel the Mamelukes and Ottomans."

'Father Athanasius disagreed with this.'

'Mu'allim Yacoub married against the rules of our orthodox faith when his wife died. The Patriarch is angry with him and does not approve of his actions and his misconduct, even with his brothers from his religion, and the Patriarch sees that his violent behaviour would bring violence to the Copts in return.'

'Violence against Copts existed before Mu'allim Yacoub, Mu'allim Yacoub wants to protect Copts from violence; when he returned from Upper Egypt and heard about killing, looting, and burning of Coptic homes, he decided that we Copts must protect ourselves. He is now training and arming Coptic youth so that they can defend us.'

'We were safe under the protection of the Sultan; the al-Ja'idiya can only be controlled by the Turks.'

'Copts are protected only by the prayers of the believers and the intercession of the Virgin May and the saints.'

The controversy continued, and many of the people of the Church were still not convinced by what the supporters of Mu'allim Yacoub were saying. Everyone went home, but many of the youth still hoped to gain more support for Mu'allim Yacoub's call for independence.

On the banks of the Nile

Julien was on a horse ride in the vast space outside Cairo with some Frenchmen. The sky was clear, and the sun flooded the earth with a pleasant warmth. He noticed from a distance a woman riding on the back of a donkey. It appeared to him that she might be Zainab, and he watched as she went towards the river Nile bank and disappeared among the dense prickly pear bushes. He left his friends under the pretext that he wanted to do a fast ride alone for a while before catching up with them in the evening. A friend said he should not be left alone, and he replied with a smile that the Egyptian resistance would not look for a French soldier in this remote place. He went alone and left his horse between the prickly pear bushes and walked down to the riverbank, following the woman, wondering if she was Zainab and what she was doing alone in this remote place.

When he saw from much closer; she was really Zainab. She put her clothes on the shore and rushed into the water naked and started playing with the waves of the Nile. After a while, she approached the shore again and rubbed her body with the black silt of the river and then rushed back into the clear waters of the Nile, her straight soft black hair floating over her shoulders. Julien moved closer, stunned and enchanted by what he saw. He watched her from his hiding place among the dense prickly pear bushes until she came out of the water, a tall, beautiful, strong, svelte, graceful brunette with a smiley face, staring at the distant horizon. Her small breasts protruded with majesty and pride, just like the queen's breasts in the statue in the temple of Luxor, but she looked more beautiful and grandiose than the Queen of Luxor, with an unbelievable charm that captivated his mind. He crept even closer but failed to notice that he was no longer hidden. Suddenly, the look in Zainab's eyes changed to a stern and determined look, and she firmly shouted at him:

'What are you doing here? Get out of my way.'

He was overcome by her presence and could not find an answer. She then screamed at him again:

'You will never be able to take me', she said with a resolute unwavering tone.

He noticed he was standing between her and her clothes, so he stepped back, giving way to her.

'Believe me, I don't want to harm you; I was just filling my eyes with your beauty; I am infatuated by your magic. What world did you come from? You belong to a world other than this world.'

She was impressed and loved what she heard and was reassured by his calm and composed voice as he did not try to touch her or approach her. Her sense of danger vanished, and she hurried to get dressed. She asked him:

'How did it happen that you knew where I was?'

'I didn't know where you were, but an enchanted little fairy guided me to you.'

She smiled and did not answer, but she liked his approach. He asked her insistently to stay with him for a while, as he just wanted to talk to her, and that if she was late, he would take her to the town gate and ask the French guards to escort her safely to her home. She became more impressed, in fact utterly delighted and surprised. The place was remote, and she tried to appear strong, but she knew that he could have raped her no matter how much she resisted or pleaded. She had never known a man who hadn't tried to take her to bed and hadn't met a man who just wanted to talk to her. She always saw lust in the eyes of men rather than respect. She now felt comfortable with Julien's gentle and friendly approach, and they sat together on the shore of the Nile. Behind them, the dense prickly pear bushes full of beautiful yellow and red fruits decorated the vast dark green overgrown bushes that separated them from the world and from what was happening in it, in front of them was the Nile flowing and the Nile Island with its dense bushes then the tall palm trees and wide green fields on the other side of the wide river. A cool and gentle late afternoon breeze caressed their faces.

They talked about Cairo for a while, and she felt more at ease with him. She told him about her late father and her love for this remote place on the shore of the Nile, which was a favourite place for him. He often took her with him on the back of his mare and they sat together on this shore. She also told him about her brother Ahmed and his dog, who never left him. Julien told her about his dog that he missed so much, about his family, his small village, Paris, the forest, the deer, as well as France and its rivers, valleys and magnificent snow-capped mountains. She was amazed and fascinated as his words touched her imagination, and she did not feel the time passing until she realised that the daylight hours were nearly gone.

Then together they heard the call of a curlew coming from afar and then saw another curlew singing nearby as if he was answering the call. Julien heard the singing of the curlew a lot in Egypt, but now he saw one for the first time in the dim light of dusk. The call of the Egyptian curlew was different from the French one. He felt these enchanting repetitive echoes in the Egyptian curlew's singing, reaching the depth of his heart and shaking it. As the curlews continued singing, Julien looked at Zainab's beautifully formed face and felt that a choir of angels was playing a celestial opera that no one had ever heard before. The sun slowly disappeared behind the horizon. The night threw its black starry veil on the vast universe, and it was time to go back.

Al-Sanadikya District, Cairo

Mansour sat alone, sipping a cup of coffee in the hall of Haj Mustafa's house. He had arrived earlier than his friends, and the servant offered him coffee while he waited. They only met occasionally anymore because the evening gathering had become difficult for some of them since the uprising. The merchants were most harmed by these events, and everyone was now trying to recover some of what was lost and repair what was destroyed. Many thoughts were circulating in his head: Bonabarta 's cannons had not destroyed his houses, but his trade was no longer what it was during the days of the Mameluke princes. He used to get many advantages from Murad Bey that he had now lost under the rule of the French. He was close to them and always provided them with useful information, but he only received a little from them in return. They had principles and rules they strictly followed, and so he no longer enjoyed the special treatment he had been used to.

What worried him most now was Murad Bey himself, who seemed to have lost much of his cunning and strength. Sari Askar the Great Bonaparte sent him the Consul of Austria in Alexandria, who was known to be a close friend of Murad Bey, with a letter saying that he would make Murad Bey the ruler of Upper Egypt in return for his submission and loyalty to the French. Murad recklessly rejected this offer, telling the Consul to go back and tell Bonaparte to gather his soldiers and return to France to protect himself from Murad Bey. Mansour was surprised at this foolish response. After all that was known about the ingenuity of the French in planning and fighting, he should have known that the French had new ways of fighting that he couldn't face and that peace with Bonaparte would allow him to return to his palaces and his slave girls. Sari Askar the Great sent a campaign to Upper Egypt to pursue Murad Bey and bring it under French control, led by one of their shrewd officers named Desaix. That Murad Bey's refusal was the beginning of a long chase which ended with Desaix retuning to Cairo victorious when Murad ended up defeated and his belongings and ammunition squandered and eventually forced to retreat south of Upper Egypt. And to make matters worse, he was only defeated after he had inflicted much damage on the people of Upper Egypt where he imposed heavy taxes on every city on his way and collected them using violence and oppression and seized from the inhabitants everything he needed by force. Mansour's means of communication with Murad Bey had been cut off, and he did not try to restore them. Perhaps the time had come for Mansour to transfer his allegiance to some other Mameluke prince who would be strong and cunning enough to handle the French, this could be al-Alfi Bey, and he had an idea how to approach him.

The friends arrived one by one, and the servants brought more coffee, cinnamon cups and hookahs. Then the chatting started:

'Desaix, the French commander in Upper Egypt, returned victorious, and Murad Bey fled to Nubia. The entire Egyptian country is now under the command of Bonabarta. Who would have believed the demise of the Mameluke princes' state?'

'The demise of their state but not their elimination. These mamelukes are too shrewd to be eliminated. Bonabarta, with all his cannons and machines could not eliminate them, Ibrahim Bey is still there in the Levant, and Murad Bey is in Nubia, ready to return as soon as the Sultan's army arrives.'

'Mu'allim Yacoub, the Coptic, went with Desaix to collect taxes for him and guide him along the roads of Upper Egypt, but he also fought with him. Yacoub now calls on all Egyptians to support the Francees so that the rule of the Mameluke princes will not return, and his ideas are spreading among people that the Egyptian country will become independent with the help of the Francees and

Egypt will become a great country as it was in the past.'

'The country's ruler cannot be a non-Muslim, and the Muslim Sultan is the caliph of all Muslims. No one will listen to Yacoub, even if some young Copts and other Christians and a few Muslims support him in what he says.'

'The Francees took al-Arwam and some Turks and Caucasians who were with Murad Bey and brought them into their military camps. They put them in French uniforms and gave them weapons and trained them in their way and organised them in their corps as they had done before with the group of Moroccans to strengthen their armies.'

'Sari Askar the Great, Prince of the Francees armies, said in a letter displayed in the markets that he had forgiven the entire people of Egypt of what happened from al- Ja'idiya of sedition and evil with the French soldiers, and he has brought back a new Diwan after it had stopped with the uprising. It became known that he was preparing to travel to the Levant to eliminate Ibrahim Bey and his Mamelukes. He will leave with a great army and will take with him managers, counsellors, translators, craftsmen, war engineers and their chief Caffarelli, the commoners called General Caffarelli "Abu Khashaba" because of his wooden artificial leg.'

'They called for the abolition of the lanterns that are lit all night in front of all houses and shops and they are to be replaced with ones in the middle of the markets and squares. Each square will have four lanterns, and the rich will pay for this, not the poor. Many people are rejoicing at their relief from this hardship.'

'The French military attacked the Arab Bedouins of al- Ayayda in the suburbs of al- Khanka, killing many of them and recovering large amounts of loot.'

'The prices of all items brought through the Mediterranean Sea increased because of the interference of English ships standing in the sea and the intensity of the Siege. Their seizure of the incoming and outgoing goods is impacting the livelihoods of many craftsmen, who are forced into lesser crafts such as selling pies and fried fish or cooking foods to be eaten in shops and cafés.'

'As for the poorest craftsmen, most of them became Makarians, the lowly donkey keepers. So many have taken up this trade that the alleyways, especially in the military areas, are crowded with donkeys offered for rent. The Francees liked this and paid generously, even if only to sit on the back of a donkey all day, riding through the streets with no need other than just the fun of riding and speeding. You can see groups of them gathering to race each other, mocking, singing and shouting at each other, with the Markarian sharing them in their fun and laughter.'

'It is the nature of the Francees to drink to the point of delight and ecstasy, and if they exceed that limit, they do not leave their homes. If one of them became drunk and went into the market to cause mischief, he would be punished for it.'

'They spend a lot of money in the markets. They pay full prices and never bargain. They are modest, not arrogant people, as is their Prince Bonabarta.

He shows affection and love and receives the sheikhs with a welcome smile.'

Mansour was careful and didn't want to praise the French in the same manner as his friends. He said before leaving:

'But they speak lewdly, and display their sins and evils, and neither do they respect Sharia laws and the religion of Islam.'

It happened in February 1799

Al-Azbakeya District, Cairo

Zainab once again knew the feeling of happiness after so many years of hardship and anguish. What had happened? What was that mysterious thrilling, and delightful feeling? It must be love, that thing that the poets write about and that she used to sing about every night without knowing what it meant. And who was this Frenchman with his peculiar foreign military uniform? How did he become the centre of her life? She couldn't stop thinking about him. Since that afternoon when he followed her to the shore of the Nile, her view of Julien and the whole world changed; she was attracted to him and no longer repelled him when he tried to get close to her. She desperately wanted him to come to see her and talk to her. She felt such pleasure talking to him, and she felt that he understood her, and that she understood him as if they had known each other for many years. She felt very much at ease with him. He understood her dreams, hopes, fears and pains. He used to frequent the restaurant with his friends a lot, but then he frequented it every day whether they came or not, and one night he stopped her while she was getting ready to go home, and she would never forget what he said:

'I love you. You are everything I could wish for from this world. Do you understand what I am saying?'

She was taken by surprise. His words did not sink in, and her mind did not help her with an answer. Julien went on:

'I don't have much time. I will go in a few days with Commander Bonaparte's campaign to the Levant, I expect to return in a few weeks, but it's war, so I may never come back. I want nothing from you except to tell me, do you share my feelings of love?'

Her mind was still unable to comprehend the situation, so she grabbed his hand and squeezed it, her eyes full of passion and affection. He then told her that the touch of her hands had magically charmed him. She gently pulled her hand away, smiling. She bid him good evening and then rushed home.

It was her habit to talk to her brother every night for a while before going to bed, but that night Ahmed smiled and told her that she was talking to him absent-mindedly. She embraced her brother tenderly and then left him and went to bed. She was finally alone and had time to calm down and reflect. Julien had surprised her. She did not know why she became bewildered by his words when she should have been prepared for it. Yes, she loved him too and was fascinated and charmed by the touch of his hand. She had never before felt such a sweeping feeling, the kind that topples the mind. It was love. She should have told him she loved him. She would the very next time she saw him.

She didn't know what to do with this love and what it meant for her life, and she needed more time to think it through, but she knew she loved him, and that was enough for now. She smiled when she thought about what her father and mother would have said if they were with her now and how her father would have reacted if he had seen Julien. Perhaps he would have said, "Who is this tall boy with weird clothes, so red-faced, and yellow-haired? Where did you get him from?" She imagined that she might have replied to her father: "It doesn't matter how he looks and if you heard him talking, you would like him and know why I love him." Yes, it was the truth; she loved him. How wonderful that feeling was.

The next day she went to work early, ecstatic and energetic, and her happiness was reflected in her talk and smiles to others. She commissioned others to do the work that needed to be done and stood behind the window waiting. She saw Julien coming from a distance with his friends. How elegant and luscious he seemed to her. She welcomed everyone into the restaurant and then signaled to him to follow her to a place where the cooks and workers could not see them. Before he uttered a word, she told him:

> 'I love you, yes, I love you, Julien, you are everything to me, didn't my eyes tell you that?'
> 'How wonderful it is to hear you say it.'

Julien's friends sat around the table waiting for food, and they watched through the window as Julien and Zainab left and strolled down towards al-Azbakeya pond, and then stood and talked in the garden on the shore of the lake in the dim light of dusk. Everyone smiled with satisfaction. They knew that their friend had what he wished for.

> 'This cunning demon Julien, he's now guaranteed to have fried pigeons stuffed with freekeh for free.'

'What a woman; lucky you Julien'

'She doesn't talk like Egyptian songstresses; she talks like an educated person.'

'Julien would have no difficulty presenting her to French society if he took her with him back to France.'

'You are assuming that she would agree to go with him. Life in Cairo is not a misery, and Egyptians are not as ignorant, stupid, or fanatical as some think. Many Egyptians, like Zainab, are eager to learn and gain knowledge if they are given the opportunity to do so.'

'You must first ask if she would agree to marry him. It seems that he is proposing marriage to her now. We will have to wait and see.'

'Wonderful news that came from members of the scientific expedition who went to Upper Egypt with General Desaix. They described and recorded so accurately what they saw of temples, buildings, statues, drawings, and graffiti so magnificent, majestic, and glorious that the simple soldiers stopped in their tracks, amazed by the outstanding greatness and solemnity of the places they saw.'

'The few antiquities of the ancient Egyptians that we saw in Cairo, Rashid, and the Delta seem to be nothing compared to what they describe in Upper Egypt.' 'Though is still nothing like the great pyramids, the largest and highest buildings in the world.'

'Also, the mosques and palaces of Cairo are magnificent.'

'The mosques and palaces of Cairo are recent and are the work of the occupiers, but these monuments are the work of the ancient Egyptians themselves, whom we do not know much about.'

'The scientists in Upper Egypt noticed that Egyptians pass red urine, and soldiers even jokingly suggested that men in Egypt were menstruating. The doctor explained to them that he thought it was caused by a disease unknown in Europe and not because Egyptians are a race of people who pass red urine.'

'The significant difference between the civilisation of the French and the backwardness of contemporary Egyptians is due to historical circumstances and not because of the nature of the

Egyptians or their religion. France was more backward and ignorant in previous centuries at a time when Egyptians were the leaders of civilisation in the world.'

'Have you heard of General Desaix's friend, whom they call Mu'allim Yacoub? He's a remarkable Egyptian.'

'What did you know about him?'

'He is a Coptic Christian tax collector who was hired by General Desaix. He was tasked with hunting down the fugitive princes in Upper Egypt. Yacoub also proved that he was a brave warrior and fought with Desaix. Yacoub has a good brain; he learned French and learned about our civilisation and the system of government in France and wants Egypt to follow our example and return to civilisation once again.'

Julien returned with Zainab, and the friends greeted them with cheering and shouting. They all kissed Zainab and wished them happiness. Zainab went to carry on with her work and supervise the preparation of dinner, and Julien remained among his friends, telling them that he had proposed to Zainab, and she had agreed. She would now have to think about how to achieve it. They talked about some other Frenchmen who had married Egyptian women, some of whom were the daughters of wealthy people. The marriage of a Frenchman to a Muslim woman without declaring conversion to Islam could lead to unrest and riots among the public, so the Frenchman had to recite the two testimonies as a declaration of conversion to Islam before the marriage took place.

During dinner, Zainab came and sat with them and talked for a while. She asked:

> 'I am impressed. Despite your young age, you know more about civilisation and science than our senior sheikhs.'
>
> 'We have been educated since childhood. We spent many years in schools, universities, and scientific institutes that gave a man knowledge.'
>
> 'I wish I could have this education. I only learned to read and write in the Kotaab. Can these schools, universities, and institutes be built in Egypt?'
>
> 'Yes, that's what Mu'allim Yacoub says. Do you know him?'
>
> 'I don't know him, but I know a lot about him. He wants this, but few listen to him. Only a few Copts

and Muslims agree with him, but most Egyptians do not understand what he says and are eager for the Francees to leave. Mu'allim Yacoub has many enemies, even within the Coptic community. Some Egyptians may be fascinated by the civilisation and progress of the Francees, but this doesn't do much good because it doesn't lead to an increase in their support for the Francees or a significant decrease in the hostility against them.'

'He's swimming against the current.'

'You can swim against the current if you're in a river, but you can't if you're facing a cataract.'

'How so?'

'Mu'allim Yacoub is imbued with your ideas and your knowledge, but it seems that Yacoub lives in one world and the rest of the Egyptians live in another, and there is no way to communicate between the two. Julien told me once about the battle of Imbaba that he remembered, when one of these mameluke cavaliers who seemed to be a majestic elder who rushed boldly towards the ranks of the French to be shot and die. The story of this man spread among the Egyptians. He was Ayoub

Bey al-Dafterdaar, the head of administration and finance in the government. In Julien's world, this man was a fool who wasted his life in a pointless act. In the Egyptian's world, they honoured him and wrote poems about his bravery, and he became a folk hero.'

'What a wonderful girl, Julien's friends said that to him when Zainab left them and returned to her work.'

Al-Sanadikya district, Cairo

Calm and tranquillity prevailed in Cairo after months of destruction, recession, and uncertainty. It was a peaceful time in Cairo and the roads were almost free of the marching soldiers of the French military, and they had even stopped patrolling streets at night. The month of Ramadan had arrived, markets and shops were open in the evening, and people came and went visiting neighbours and friends even at night. They walked with lanterns and even without them and met in cafés and mosques and prayed Taraweeh prayers. The sound of al-Mesaharaty's drum returned to the lanes. Just before Dawn al-Mesaharaty, walked the streets beating his drum to wake people up to have a meal before fasting all day.

Trade flourished, and prices fell except for the scarce goods from other countries unavailable due to the British blockade of Egypt's seaports.

Egyptian families returned to what they used to do in the month of Ramadan: they received the holy month with joy, decorated their homes with flags, and lit them at night with lanterns. Ramadan is when the evenings are filled with visits to each other's homes, and the rich give cooked food in many large bowls and distribute them to the poor and needy. Cairenes go to the Nile shore in Boulaq, where there are many cafés for people to gather in. They celebrate by dancing, singing, and listening to poets singing the biographies of folk heroes while playing his Rababa, a single-string musical instrument. It was the custom of these cafés to close their doors all day during Ramadan, and only open them after Iftar in the evening. And so during the holy month, commoners would first conduct al-Taraweeh prayers, then go to sit in the cafes and enjoy the entertainment until two or three o'clock in the morning.

The French invited to their banquets notable people, such as sheikhs and wealthy merchants to share the two meals of the day during Ramadan with them, these were Iftar and Suhoor. The French followed Muslim customs in their banquets and made sure to bring Muslim cooks and waiters to these banquets to reassure the Egyptians, because it was commonly thought among the public at this time that the French were trying to poison Muslims. The French also were invited by senior Sheikhs, and they went to their houses, ate Iftar with them, and watched their arrangements and habits. People found the French to be well-mannered, kind, and modest.

People talked about a particular Frenchman, the governor of the Scene of Al Husseini district, whom they found to be considerate and tolerant. They saw him showing love for Muslims and being kind to them. He entered the houses of the neighbours with respect. He respected and venerated the ulema and Islamic Jurists and honoured them by accepting their demands when they pleaded on behalf of the district's residents. He took armed French soldiers off the streets, and he disciplined those who were too strict in maintaining order. The people of the Scene of Al Husseini were reassured and began to attend al-Fajr prayers in the mosques again after they had stopped doing so because of their fear of the French soldiers. Because of him, they returned to their habit and walked at night without panic or fear, and they began to meet with him to talk, joke, and have fun. He even began to bring his wife to social gatherings, who was the daughter of one of the deposed Mamelukes.

People noticed the French movements with interest as they prepared to travel to the Levant. They began to prepare camels, mules, and donkeys to carry their supplies, food, and ammunition, and tow their cannons. Sari Askar the Great called the Diwan and told the sheikhs that he would be absent for a month and told them to ensure they maintained control of the country and the community in his absence and ensure that they told the district governors to ensure they maintained discipline in their areas as well. If they did they would avoid conflict with the French military forces that remained in Egypt.

An atmosphere of jubilation returned to the gathering of friends in the house of Haj Mustafa, the owner of the big house in al-Sanadikya. They started talking as they had before, in a mood of comfort and safety. Mansour sat among them, sharing the sarcasm, laughter, hookah, coffee, and cinnamon drink cups, but he could not share his feelings with them. Each of them talked, their mind at ease, so they spoke about work, family, children and grandchildren, but Mansour alone kept his secrets and couldn't speak about what he kept deep in himself. Everyone seemed to have forgotten the months of destruction and turmoil in the recent past and regained their peace of mind, except Mansour who never felt that way. Ever since the fleeing of the Mameluke princes and Bekir Pasha, he felt insecure and did not trust the French's ability to control Egypt.

The usual discussion took place, but Mansour was inattentive:

> 'Bonabarta took large numbers of camels, mules, and donkeys to carry ammunition and supplies with him to the Levant. The Sheikhs and governors of the neighbourhoods were ordered to collect them from the people, and now the people face hardship because of it.'
>
> 'Bonabarta had taken al-Arish and Gaza from the Turks and Mamelukes, but Sultan's army is waiting for him in Syria to eliminate him. The decisive battle has not yet taken place. After eliminating the French army in the Levant, the way will be open for the Sultan's army to come and rid the Egyptian country of the Franks. The Sultan's army will come from land and sea, and what is left of the Francees will not be able to hold on.'

'The Francees are formidable at war. The Arab Bedouins of Sinai who saw them fighting said that the castle of al-Arish could not hold out long despite all that al-Gezzar Pasha did to strengthen and fortify it. The Sultan sent many soldiers and a lot of equipment to strengthen al-Gezzar, but no one seems able to beat them.'

'Sari Askar took managers, counsellors, translators, craftsmen such as blacksmiths, carpenters, war engineers, and their chief Abu Khashaba who surpasses everyone in know-how and knowledge.'

'Their weapons, their systems in war, and their cannons are invincible.'

'Murad Bey and those with him kept fleeing south, and whenever the French soldiers approached them, they retreated further because of their great fear of facing the French.'

'The English also have the know-how and knowledge, and they have allied with the Sultan against the Francees, and the English boats in the Sea of Al-Room (Mediterranean Sea) are helping al-Gezzar Pasha.'

'The English also have a religion. Unlike the Francees, who have no religion, they are Christians. Why would Christians help the Sultan?'

'Interests are what make events; alliances are not shaped by religious beliefs as much as they are shaped by interests.'

'The Francees superiority in most things and their scientific advances have not much changed how Egyptians view them.'

'They flew a large French balloon again at al-Azbakeya pond, intending to dazzle the people who gathered at noon to watch, and it flew and climbed into the air and sailed over the hills of al-Barkiya before it fell. If there had been some wind, it would have pushed it farther away until it disappeared from view. The people would have believed that it could travel to distant countries.'

'During the festival of al-Fitre, the Francees leaders rode among the notables and sheikhs of the country and congratulated them on the celebration, and the people were polite to them in return.'

'When the men and women visited Al-Nasr cemetery, as was the custom during the feast about the areas of Al Nasr graveyard, some of al-Ja'idiya shouted at them, saying, "the Arab Bedouin are about to attack you!" Some people began to panic and run away, and in the confusion, al-Ja'idiya swooped in and stole their clothes and jewellery of women and the turbans of men. The press of bodies trying to escape the imaginary bandits caused some women to fall to the ground and they were underfoot by the crowd. The Bedouin's attack was not true, but al-Ja'idiya bastards invented that for the purpose of stealing.'

'Al-Ja'idiya would not dare to do that in the presence of the French soldiers.'

'The Francees love justice. They killed three members of their own military, executed them with bullets in the field under the castle, and rebuked Daluy, the governor of the Calipha district. They ordered his imprisonment in the castle because of what was done to Prince Zulfiqaar and the grain merchants.'

'Also, Sari Askar the Great punished those who abused the house of Sheikh Mohammed al-Gohary, killing two of them and lowering a group from their high status to the lowest status.'

'Even that hasn't changed the public's view of the Francees. They see them as flattering Egyptians for their own malicious purposes.'

The church

Priest Athanasius began Mass by putting on his decorated vestments, the design of which had not changed over centuries, and making the sign of the cross while reciting the Psalms. In the atmosphere of peace and stability that prevailed in Cairo, the church was crowded with worshippers, and the priest and deacons went on to recite the Coptic mass. The people of the church repeated the words of the verses and prayers with them until the priest announced the end of the mass, singing in Coptic melody, "Because he is blessed and filled with glory, your Holy Name, Father and Son, and Holy Spirit, now and in all times, and to the end of all times, amen." The congregation lined up for the holy communion, and the priest blessed them with a sprinkle of holy water. Some stayed to talk to the priest, and others walked away chatting with each other:

'Mu'allim Yacoub returned to Cairo after the campaign in Upper Egypt. When he learned of the killings and the looting of Christian homes during the Cairo revolution, he rushed to turn his house into something like a military castle and made a fortified gate outside of which armed guards stood, day and night. This coincided with Sari Askar the Great beginning to construct several castles around Cairo so that his cannons surrounded the whole city. The castle of the Mu'allim Yacoub looks similar to those of the Francees.'

'Mu'allim Yacoub's actions provoked the anger of Muslims against Christians, and the Francees sympathised with the Muslims at the expense of the Christians, so the Christians have become oppressed between the two of them.'

'A sheikh passed by a Christian smoking on the day of Ramadan, and he rebuked him. The Christian replied to him, and that angered the Sheikh, who went down and rebuked and hit the Christian, and the people gathered around him. The governor of the district came and raised the issue to the French mayor who asked the Christians present about their customs in that. They told him that one of their old customs is that during the month of Ramadan, they would not eat or drink in the markets or in front of any Muslim at all. The mayor then ordered the beating of the Christian and left the sheikh to go, so this poor Christian was beaten by both the Muslims and the Francees.'

'The Francees warned people, saying that in Ramadan the country's Christians follow their customs with Muslims by not eating and not drinking or smoking in front of Muslims. It is not wise for Christians to boast and show pleasure in their liberation from the restrictions imposed on them by the Mameluke princes because that provokes the anger of Muslims. Mu'allim Yacoub must be careful to maintain the peace that exists between Christians and Muslims.'

Al-Husseiniya district, Cairo

There was great discussion around Sheikh Abd al-Rahman in the mosque about how infuriated the brotherhood was after receiving of news from the Levant regarding the victories of Bonaparte. They were also angry that the Copts and al-

Shwam in Egypt showed pleasure at the news of the triumph of the French in al-Arish and Gaza, and they held banquets to celebrate with increased ugliness and heinousness. The infuriation of the Brotherhood multiplied even further when the French requested that the sheikhs fly al-Arish victory banners on the minarets of Al-Azhar, and they complied.

Sheikh Abd al-Rahman told the men gathered around him in the mosque about the need for believers to be patient and to wait for the right time for jihad and that the lack of wisdom harms Muslims. He told them about a Moroccan man who was called Sheikh Kilani who was an associate in Mecca, Medina and al-Taif; when the news of French taking Egypt reached the Hijaz. This disturbed the people of Hijaz, so much that he called them to jihad and incited them to support righteousness and the religion. People agreed, and many volunteered to fight while others donated money. Sheikh Kilani gathered about six hundred mujahideen and sailed to al-Kosair where a group of the people of Upper Egypt and some Turks and Moroccans and some from Gaza who had fought at the battle of Imbaba, joined them. Kilani and his small army fought the French but were defeated and fled. Their impetuous action did not help Muslims.

Hussein joined the others in prayer and listened to their conversation, but he was distracted by his thoughts. He had returned home after a day of hard work. As peace and stability prevailed in Cairo, his business and trade flourished, and orders continued to come to his workshop. His wife Suoad had yet to return from visiting her mother. He went and talked to his father, as he used to do every day, to tell him about the goings on at work and the tasks he was assigned to perform. Afterwards, he went to his room alone, and the maid brought him a cup of coffee. He read a book of Islamic jurisprudence, waiting for the call to have dinner with his family.

He was still unsettled, anxious and disappointed, as he couldn't find peace of mind. His marriage to Suoad did not bring comfort and peace as he had hoped, and Suoad knew little about him and did not know or did not understand his thoughts and feelings. Their bodies came together, united and adhered, but their souls did not meet. She did not talk to him except about the affairs of the house. She was a virtuous and chaste Muslim who followed all her religious duties, but she did not understand jurisprudence or Sharia laws and did not even try to know. Discussion with her was just naïve talk, superficial, and did not delve into any depth. She knew nothing about the danger posed by the Francees nor the necessity to expel them from the land of Muslims. She did everything she could to please him but also didn't talk about how she felt, as her modesty prevented her from talking about her emotions. He both lived with her and apart from her. And worst of all, his marriage to her didn't help him stop thinking about Zainab. He still loved Zainab and still remembered the sweet memories of his childhood and adolescence with her. He was still trying to know everything he could about Zainab. He knew where her new house was, and also about where the food house she owned and managed. He also knew that a French officer wanted to marry her, and so he investigated further until he found this officer, who lived near Zainab's house. He couldn't talk to anyone about his agony and torment; it was his hidden secret. His friends and his mentor Sheikh Abd al-Rahman would not understand or accept that he still clung to Zainab. He felt from his mother's gaze that she knew what he was hiding deep inside. She rebuked him many times when she noticed that he did not speak kindly to Suoad and repeatedly spoke in front of him about Zainab's immorality and debauchery.

Thinking about what might happen to Zainab after the demise of the French, he wondered if she might return to religion and righteousness so that it would be possible for him to marry her. He and his peers were preparing to fight the French when the Sultan's army came, and they hid weapons for that time. He learned to use guns and had even become skilled at it. He hoped that, when the hour of Jihad came, he would be able to kill that French infidel who wanted to marry Zainab.

Gaza, Palestine

Julien sat among a group of officers at the French camp in Gaza. They had some time to rest before resuming the campaign to the north towards Damascus; and had plenty of food, drink, supplies, and ammunition. They brought some lighter cannons with them, but the heavy guns were loaded in ships that sailed to meet the expedition on the coast of the Holy Land.

It was an arduous journey through the desert to reach Gaza, Bonaparte's army of 13,000 men, with their equipment and ammunition, began the journey to Suez, and then they took the coastal road beside the Red Sea until it reached the Well of Moses. After a short rest, the expedition moved again when the Red Sea was at low tide, but they lost their way and were caught by the high tide. They were left walking and dragging their cannons on a swamp-like road, which was very difficult. The situation began to look like the sinking of the army of the Pharaoh of Egypt in the Red Sea when he was chasing Moses and the Jewish people. For the second time, Julien faced the hardship of crossing the desert, but this time it was less complicated due to the fair winter weather. Bonaparte had no difficulty in capturing the castle at al-Arish, which surrendered after they began to fire their cannons at the walls. Bonaparte's army also had no problem in capturing Gaza and Khan Yunis.

It happened in May 1799

Acre, Palestine

From atop the Tigre, anchored in the port of Acre, Admiral Sidney Smith stood looking with satisfaction at the heavy cannons firing from the fortified walls of the fortress of Acre. In the distance, the army of Napoleon Bonaparte began to retreat at twilight as darkness approached. Bonaparte had finally decided to break the siege of Acre and leave after nine weeks, during which Sidney Smith was able to thwart nine major attacks and three smaller ones as the French tried to capture the city. What a wonderful sense of victory he felt as he watched the French army slowly withdrawing south. Bonaparte now would have no choice but to return to Egypt with what was left of his embattled army. The Christians in Lebanon and Syria did not cooperate and revolt against the Ottoman Sultan as Bonaparte had hoped because Sidney Smith had sent them copies of the statement that Napoleon wrote to the Muslims of Egypt in which he showed his love of Islam and hostility to the Christian Pope, so Smith won the loyalty of Christians. It would not be difficult now to completely expel the French from all the vast territories that Bonaparte had seized in the Levant campaign. Sidney Smith had succeeded in eliminating the French threat to British interests in the Levant. The Mediterranean would become a British lake.

This new victory would undoubtedly strengthen his position in the Royal Navy despite Nelson's enmity towards him. He did a lot to deserve respect. After the French Revolution, when England became an enemy of France, he participated in the attempt to destroy the French fleet in the port of Toulon, in cooperation with French royalists. Things did not go well, and he was captured, along with his secretary in Normandy, though after two years in a French prison, he managed to escape with the help of French royalists. After the Battle of Abu Qir, he became captain of the Tigre, a French ship captured during the Battle that became part of the British fleet.

Two days before Napoleon arrived at Acre, Sidney Smith and the French military engineer Antoine de Filippo, who was now fighting with the British, arrived with the two English ships - Theseus and Tigre - and anchored in the port of Acre with the aim of preventing Napoleon from seizing it. Antoine de Filippo was a colleague of Bonaparte but had turned against him after the revolution and helped Sidney Smith escape from prison and was now fighting against Bonaparte and the Army of the Republic. Sidney Smith was able to supply al-Gezzar Pasha with the necessities and ammunition he needed by sea, so Napoleon's siege failed to cut off his supplies and force him to surrender. Sidney Smith could not believe his luck when he saw nine French ships carrying the big cannons and other supplies for Napoleon arrive in port. He surprised them and captured six of them, depriving Napoleon of the big cannons needed to break Acre's fortified walls, and then used these French cannons to strengthen the defences of the Acre by directing them to bomb the French. With the help of the heavy guns and two hundred of his sailors and soldiers, Sidney Smith spoilt Napoleon's repeated attempts to break Acre's defences. No one could doubt the magnitude of what he was able to accomplish. Without his help, al-Gezzar Pasha could not have withstood Napoleon's siege for more than few days.

Bonaparte's armies around Acre disappeared from sight, night came, and the moon illuminated the earth that was otherwise plunged in darkness. Sidney Smith contemplated the splendour, grandeur, and beauty of the full moon, which appeared as a King crowned on the throne of the sky, which increased his sense of comfort and contentment.

Jaffa, Palestine

Julien stood alone on the seashore under the moonlight, the army withdrew from Acre. They are now on their way back to Cairo, many of his peers did not feel defeated and felt that the Levant campaign had achieved many victories. The main goal of the campaign was to prevent the Sultan's army from invading Egypt, which they achieved. There was no need to take Acre, but he still felt distraught, he felt the feeling of those who fought with a defeated army.

After the capture of Gaza, the expedition proceeded on its planned path until it reached Jaffa, Napoleon sent a messenger to the governor of Jaffa offering him safety if he agreed to surrender, but the response was to behead his messenger and hang his head on the city wall. The French were outraged and attacked the city, and when the infuriated French soldiers entered the city, they fought brutally until the Turkish garrison defending the city surrendered. Julien saw brutality in the treatment of the inhabitants of Jaffa and watched in disbelief as the French soldiers led their Turkish captives to the seashore to execute them. Their orders were to use their bayonets to kill them in order to save gunpowder. Julien watched the massacre unfold before his eyes, the surrendered Turkish soldiers throwing themselves into the sea to escape bullets and stabbing, where many of them drowned. Only a few managed to swim out to reach some rocks, but they could not escape. The French soldiers in boats rowed out to them and killed them to the last man.

Many of his colleagues understood why they killed their captives on the basis that Commander Bonaparte had no other choice. He faced many enemies: not only the Mamelukes, Turks and English but also the villagers and Arabs Bedouins. There was no way to keep three thousand prisoners of war with them or to transport them to Egypt and if they were released they would join the Sultan's army and fight again. Some said that the response of the governor of Jaffa to

Napoleon's message by beheading the French messenger was enough to justify the massacre. Either argument might be true, but Julien wondered if Bonaparte would have done this to the prisoners of war if they were Europeans. Was this consistent with the revolution's principles of equality? Julien questioned whether the revolution had really changed anything because he saw the army of the French Republic undervaluing the lives of those who were not Europeans. Many officers of the aristocracy in France did not value the lives of their soldiers because they were commoners. The killing of captives tarnished France's reputation, as no one would trust the morals of the French in the future, and it provided a reason to treat French prisoners of war in the same way.

As the campaign reached the fields around Acre, Napoleon stood in his command post on a hill to watch with dismay as the French ships carrying siege equipment and heavy guns were captured by Sidney Smith. Julien knew that the cannons that were supposed to help capture Acre would not arrive, and that the light cannons they had transported by land had no power to make a breach in the wall. Also, the plague had spread amongst soldiers since the battle in Jaffa. This added another difficulty for the commander. Julien wondered if this plague was divine justice for what the French did to the people of Jaffa and their Turkish prisoners.

At the beginning of his siege of the castle of Acre, Napoleon sent General Kleber at the head of a force of two thousand soldiers to Marj Ibn Amer. Their task was to repel a possible attack from the east, and this attack materialised, it came from the Turkish forces that arrived from the Levant to help repel the siege of Acre. Kleber's forces were able to defeat them, but new Turkish forces arrived and joined the forces of the Sultan in attacking Kleber between Mount Tabor and the town of Foula using hit-and-run attacks. They continued until Kleber's forces almost ran out of ammunition, at which point Napoleon arrived with a relief force. The situation changed as he bombarded the Turks with cannons. Julien was with this force, and they fought valiantly until they forced the Turks to flee to the mountains around the city of Jenin. Napoleon followed them, burned Jenin and its neighbouring villages, and then returned to Acre. Julien participated in many of the victories of the Levant campaign, but that did not diminish his sorrow at the events in Jaffa.

One evening, Julian stood alone looking at the moon among the stars in the sky, and contemplating; it was the same moon that flooded all sides of the earth with its light and connected countries no matter how far the distances between them. He marvelled at how beautiful the light was in the midst of the darkness, and how it filled the earth with joy and wonder and eliminated sorrow and sadness. The moon awakened in him feelings of splendour and beauty. Zainab told him before leaving to look up to the moon whenever he could so that the moon might convey to him the feelings of her heart and the magnitude of her longings and love. She told him to send his return messages through the moon as it could reach her. Could Zainab also be at this moment looking at the moon, contemplating him? Could the moon tell her how much he missed her and longed to see her? She was not like any girl he'd ever known. She had not only a beautiful face and a sweet voice, she was his soul mate. She seemed very intelligent, she understood him and his feelings as if he'd known her for years. She shared with him the sense of the beauty of nature and the creatures of the earth, whether plants, animals or birds. She loved dogs as he did, and she once told him that she was fascinated by looking into her dog's eyes. Her brother Ahmed's dog could understand what she wanted just by looking at her eyes and facial expressions. She saw loyalty, sincerity, and love by looking into her dog's eyes.

When she agreed to marry him, he felt that he had the world and everything in it. It was the kind of happiness that people crave and don't get. He hadn't felt that emotion with any other girl he knew before, and he wanted to spend the rest of his life with her. Everything else in his life fell to second place and Zainab became the most important thing in his life. But how to get her? And how could a Catholic marry a Muslim? He didn't know the answer but he would find out. She handled her sexual instincts differently from the French girls he knew because of her Egyptian upbringing. He wouldn't risk upsetting her but instead would let her choose the way and time to express her desires that suited her. He could take her to France. She had nothing to connect her to Egypt other than her brother and they could all live together in his small village outside Paris. He would be proud of her and with her in his life, he would feel fully contented.

Al-Sanadikya district, Cairo

While the fierce battles were raging in the Holy Land, things were quiet in Cairo. Peace and stability still prevailed, and the pace of life continued on as if nothing had happened. When peace prevails and conflict stops, trade, crafts and industry flourish, and wealth increases. The British blockade of the ports had reduced the trade of some, but the wealthy merchants found other ways to profit. Only scattered news came from the Levant until the French wounded arrived with news that the war was still going on between them and al-Gezzar Pasha and that the chief architect of their army Abu Khashaba had died. The French grieved because he was one of their most shrewd, inventive, and courageous men and had a deep knowledge of the best management of wars and the place of fighting and the knowledge of buildings and how to besiege castles and take them. Mansour sat amongst Haj Ibrahim and his friends enjoying peace and carrying on their usual chats, stories, jokes and laughter, and then the conversation turned serious when touched on the events that were taking place around them:

> 'Strife had occurred in the Damanhour region because a Moroccan man claimed he was the Mahdi, the anticipated saviour and leader of all Muslims, and called for people to rise up inciting them to jihad. Then al-Alfi Bey came to Damanhour and the Arab Bedouins gathered around him and fought the Francees but were

defeated. Al-Alfi also came to Sharqia, fought the Francees there as well, and fled.'

'The feast of al-Adha passed without the required sacrifices because all the livestock was quarantined, and people were too busy to find alternatives.'

'The Francees used a line of wooden boats to make a bridge from the land of Cairo near Qasr El-Aini to al-Rowda and then to Giza, which made it easier for people to cross the Nile from Cairo to Giza.'

'The English whispered about the death of Bonabarta and the demise of his army in the Levant and that rumour spread quickly among the public.'

'Little news came about Bonabarta's army in the Levant. A letter from Sari Askar the Great arrived to the sheikhs of the Diwan, telling them about his taking of Jaffa and his siege of Acre and that he forgave the people of Egypt who were taking refuge in Jaffa. He reassured them and ordered their honoured safe return to Egypt. Among them was Omar Makram Effendi, the former leader of the nobles, and other Effendies who had fled to the

Levant with Ibrahim Bey. It was then reported that Omar Makram Effendi and his companions had arrived safely in Damietta and returned to their homes.'

'These men were sheltering in the castle in Jaffa, but when the Francees captured the castle and the town, they did not harm the Egyptians. Sari Askar the Great sent for them and chastised them for their escape from Egypt, but he then gave them decent clothes and sent them to Damietta by sea.'

'They sent the flags and banners that they took from the Citadel of Jaffa to al-Azhar Mosque. They took down the flags of al-Arish Citadel that had been flying on the high minarets of al-Azhar and raised the banners of Jaffa instead.'

'The interruption of news about the Francees besieging Acre has caused gossip to spread everywhere.'

'Sari Askar the Great sent another letter saying they were preparing to enter the castle of Acre and that they had conquered the Sultan's army as it came from Damascus to fight him at Mount Tabor.'

'This news about Bonabarta defeating the Sultan's army at Mount Tabor was found to be true, yet many people did not believe that Bonabarta could do so.'

'What happened had happened; it doesn't seem that the demise of the state of the Francees might happen soon.'

'It will happen soon when the Sultan's other army comes by sea.'

'They also arranged that printed orders were posted in the markets and lanes regarding the plague. The Francees ordered everyone to report sick people and that those who did not report them would be subject to the maximum penalty. People were also ordered to report the arrival of any guest or traveller arriving from another district or province. The disease spreading in the Levant was also spreading in Alexandria, and they knew how to limit its spread. They placed the plagued in quarantine and also quarantined those who contacted or cared for them.'

'People hate quarantine more than death.'

Mansour was following the arguments and talking as if he was sure of the victory of the Sultan and the princes and the demise of the French, but deep down; he felt bewilderment and turmoil. He no longer saw in Murad Bey that strong man who could lead, but he found these qualities in al-Alfi Bey, who seemed more cunning in dealing with the Franks and their army in a hit-and-run manner, so they could never catch him. Mansour was able to communicate with al-Alfi secretly and told him about the conditions of the community and the Egyptian countryside and how people yearned for salvation from the Francees, Mansour wished that the state of the Mameluke princes would return and predicted that if this happened, it would be al-Alfi and not Murad Bey in the forefront position. But he also saw the impossibility of this for now in light of the superiority of the French and their unsurpassed strength.

While sitting on the garden terrace, the friends noticed the moonlight flooding the jasmine bushes, which only added more charm to their beautiful flowers and breathtaking fragrance:

> 'The moon adorns the sky at night, stirring feelings of beauty.'
> 'It fills the earth with pleasure and gratification.'

'No wonder they say that a beautiful girl is like the moon.'

Al-Husseiniya district, Cairo

The French's orders hung on the markets and lanes regarding the plague sparked outrage among Hussein and his peers as they saw this as an attack on the privacy and sanctity of Muslims. None of them were convinced that these orders could limit the spread of the plague. They saw searching houses as nothing but a trick whose purpose was to know the secrets of Muslims so that they could eliminate them. They held high hopes that the Sultan's Army would eliminate Bonaparte and disperse his army in the Levant. Few conflicting news reached them from the Arab Bedouins about Bonaparte's taking of the Jaffa Citadel and the siege of Acre and his victory over the Sultan's army in the Levant. They didn't believe any of it. When this news was later confirmed to be true, they were amazed as they thought Bonaparte's victory was impossible, especially in that short period.

Sheikh Abd al-Rahman missed giving the evening lesson, and the Brotherhood dispersed to their homes after Isha prayers.

In the narrow street and in the dim light of the oil lantern, Hussein noticed the radiance of the moon amid the darkness of the sky, and without thinking about it, the image of his beloved Zainab's face appeared to him in its light. The moon had a charm that renewed hope in souls and immersed hearts in passion. He started reciting verses from the Qur'an "And He subjected for you the night and the day, and the sun, the moon, and the stars are subjected to His command. Indeed, in that are signs for people who understand.", "And the sun, the moon, and the stars are subjected to His command. Surely His is the creation and the command, blessed be God, Lord of the worlds. the truth of the great God."

The church

Priest Athanasius concluded the evening mass and then spoke to the congregation gathered around him about the importance of prayer and trust in God. He said that anxiety about the world's affairs came from a lack of faith and read to them what the Apostle Paul had said: "Don't worry about anything, but in all your prayers ask God for what you need always asking him with a thankful heart and God's peace which is far beyond human understanding, will keep your hearts and minds safe in union with Christ Jesus."

On the way home the conversation revolved around existing affairs. One man mentioned that a Christian Shamy, from the Levant, who passed through the scene of al-Husseini riding on a donkey, was stopped and ordered to dismount in honour of the scene as usual, by a Muslim translator for the district governor named al-Said Abdullah. The Christian refused, and then Abdullah rebuked him and beat him and threw him to the ground. The Christian went to the French and complained to them, they arrested Abdullah and imprisoned him. The Christian brought someone who testified that al-Said Abdullah was reckless in his act. The Christian claimed that he lost six thousand dirhams that were in his pocket when he was beaten, so they kept the translator in prison until he paid him back. No Christian was treated so fairly in the days of the Mameluke princes.

Then they talked about the news from the Levant that Bonaparte had overcome the Sultan's army and the prevailing belief among them was the superiority of the French and the permanence of their state in the Egyptian Land, but their feelings about it conflicted between those who believed that the French lifted injustice from the Copts and those who believed only the princes and the Sultan could protect the Copts from al-Ja'idiya and the lower classes. Some men stressed the need to maintain friendliness with Muslims and in the middle of the discussion someone noticed the splendour of the moon in the middle of the sky:

> 'How bright and beautiful is the moon in the sky, moving behind the clouds, praise God the creator and adjuster of all.'
> 'Devine eternal light is a pleasure to watch.'
> 'The glory of God and the light of God illuminate the world, praise God, O sun and moon, praise him, all the planets of light.'

Al-Azbakia district, Cairo

Friends sat around the dinner table in the restaurant talking. Zainab was always asking about Julien and asking them to try to find out about him. Even though they didn't get any news from him, they knew from others some news about what was happening on the battlefield. The letters of Bonaparte spoke of a series of victories and that he was about to take Acre after capturing al-Arish, Gaza and Jaffa, defeating and dispersing the Sultan's army in the Holy Land

and reaching as far north as the city of Tyre. But it was not all good news, as they also heard that the campaign was facing many difficulties at Acre, and they learned that some of their colleagues had been killed and that General Caffarelli had been seriously injured, and they did not know if Julien was alive. They also learned that the cannons and equipment sent by sea had fallen into the hands of the British, and they regretted that Julien was fighting without the heavy cannons that he had much skill and experience in using. Their scientific work in Cairo was going very well and they succeeded in accomplishing everything they were assigned to do. Things were quiet in Cairo and people were enjoyed a period of peace, in sharp contrast to what was happening in the Levant. The friends said:

> 'There are many accounts of what is happening in the Levant, but most of them come from unreliable sources.'
>
> 'News of a plague outbreak among French soldiers is probably true.'
>
> 'The Turks cannot face the superiority and excellence of Bonaparte, but they seek the help of the English and the Russians'

'The British seem to have succeeded in defending Acre, but the goal of the campaign was achieved by destroying the Turkish army and preventing it from invading Egypt.'

'Some messages arrived, but nothing has come from Julien, and Zainab keeps asking about him.'

Zainab returned home after another day of hard work and talked for some time with her brother Ahmed. She found him smiling as usual, which gave her a feeling of comfort. She used to open her heart to him when talking about the events of her day, and after some hesitation, she revealed to him her feelings for Julien. What she feared most was that this revelation would disturb his serenity. It was a great relief and comfort to her when she found him agreeing with her and wishing her happiness. How meek and tender Ahmed was.

She went to bed exhausted, tired, and preoccupied. Frogs peeping and singing of curlews and crickets interrupted the tranquillity of the night in al-Azbakeya. She went to the open window to breathe in the cool, fresh night air to calm her soul. She had lived alone for a long time and had become used to it, but now that she had found a companion to her heart and soul, she felt the cruelty of loneliness for the first time. She looked at the moon shining in the middle of the sky, illuminating the darkness of the night and throwing delight on trees, palms, streets, squares and palaces around the al-Azbakeya pond, and scattering its silver rays of light to her through the window. She felt and wished from within that Julien was alive and that he contemplated the moon that connected them despite the vast deserts, valleys and mountains that separated them. The moon rose with splendour as it moved silently across the sky. Ooh, how wonderful it was, she thought. The moon was her companion in her loneliness in the darkness of the night. Could the moon convey to Julien the feelings within her? Could the moon tell him how much she missed him, longed to see him, and couldn't wait to throw herself into his embrace?

It happened in June 1799

Bab al-Nasr, Cairo

Messengers arrived with news of the arrival of Bonaparte and his army in al-Salihia on the way to Cairo. Deputy Sari Askar Dugua who was in charge of the French army in Egypt, sent directions to the sheikhs, notables, leaders, and the people of Cairo to go out to meet him. At dawn, they gathered in al-Azbakeya with torches, drums, horns, and various Turkish musical instruments. They marched to al-Adliya where they all met the Great Sari Askar Bonaparte and greeted him. From Bab al-Nasr (the gate of victory), they followed him and his army back to the city. The cannons fired when the huge procession entered Cairo, a long line of soldiers, drums, horns, horses, carts, women, and children. It took Bonaparte nearly five hours of the day to reach his home in al-Azbakeya.

Al-Sanadikya district, Cairo

Naaman Al Roomy, a Greek orthodox man and Saad Allah the Coptic arrived early at Haj Mustapha's house when everyone else was participating in a congregational Isha prayer, so they waited in the patio area for the others. When they had finished their prayer and the supplications that followed, they came, and everyone sat around the hookahs, coffee and cinnamon cups. The conversation was about the news that people everywhere were talking about, which was the return of Bonaparte from the Levant:

> 'Bonabarta had already written from the Levant to say that he had decided to return to Egypt and that he had destroyed al-Gezzar's palace and demolished the walls of Acre and did not leave a stone untouched. All its inhabitants had been defeated and escaped to the sea road and al-Gezzar was wounded. He fled with his harem and followers to a tower by the seaside and he was in danger of death.'

> 'Despite everything Bonabarta says, everyone understood the French failed to take Acre after weeks of siege and repeated attacks day and night, and Ahmed Pasha al-Gezzar and his soldiers did well and some of the Francees testified to this.'

'They had sent to the sheikhs, notables, leaders, and others to join Dugua the Deputy Sari Asker, and the French senior officers and their soldiers in greeting the great Sari Askar Bonabarta. They entered Cairo with him from Bab al-Nasr gate in a huge procession that railed behind him until he reached his home in al-Azbakeya, at which point the crowd broke up. The cannons were firing as they entered the city.'

'Sheikhs of the Diwan wrote a leaflet, that was printed and distributed in the markets and lanes regarding the return of Bonabarta in an enormous, splendid procession, accompanied by scholars, leaders, notables, and wealthy Egyptian merchants. The leaflet described it as a great day and said Bonabarta was admired by all. In the leaflet the sheikhs said the people of Egypt went out to meet him when they found him, the great prince himself, it became clear that the rumours about his demise were lies. That sheikh's leaflet went on to say God endeared him to Islam and those who spread false news were Arab bandits and immoral and corrupt fugitives and what they wanted to achieve by these rumours was the destruction of the land of Islam and Muslim people.'

'The sheikhs of the Diwan also wrote leaflets, printed them and posted them in markets everywhere, in which they claimed that the great Sari Askar loved the religion of Islam, glorified the Prophet, peace be upon him, respected the Qur'an and read from it every day perfectly. They said he ordered the establishment of Islamic mosques for the people of Egypt that had no equal in any other country, and that he entered the religion of the chosen prophet, the best prayer and peace be upon him.'

'Amusement parks, clowns, magicians, monkey shows, and dancers gathered around the house of Sari Askar the Great in al-Azbakeya and set up swings as they do during holidays and seasons, and they continued like that for three days. Sari Askar eventually paid them baksheesh, gratuity money, and then they left.'

'Omar Makram Effendi, the former leader of the nobles, came from Damietta to Cairo. He was taking refuge in Jaffa when Bonabarta entered and he was one of those who went down from Jaffa to the sea to return to Egypt. Some dignitaries went to meet Omar Makram and went with him to his house. The next day they went with Sheikh al-Mahdi and met Sari Askar, who welcomed Omar Makram, promised him safety and returned some of his belongings.'

Mansour knew that the English had allied themselves with al-Gezzar Pasha, which was the reason why Bonaparte failed to take Acre and that the English were preparing to attack Egypt with the Sultan's army. It was the English who could match the superiority of the French. This alliance could overcome the French' superiority and could lead to the return of the Mameluke princes' rule. Murad Bey and Ibrahim Bey were defeated, but al-Alfi Bey was still maintaining his power and would be the ruler of Egypt when the armies of the Sultan arrived. Mansour was now certain that he must approach al-Alfi and work with him.

Al-Azbakeya district, Cairo

Many rumours had spread that Bonaparte had been killed in the Levant, so people came to meet him to check for themselves, and in the middle of the crowd, Zainab kept watching the long line of returnees looking for Julien. Until this time, she was not sure that he was still alive, and then she spotted him from afar, he was Julian himself among the officers and soldiers. The strong beating of her heart shook her chest, as she was overwhelmed with joy. She waved to him with her hand and he noticed her and waved as well. Despite her pleasure at seeing him, she noticed that they must have endured great hardship, as their clothes appeared dull and torn, and some were without hats or shoes. Julien disappeared into the crowd with the rest on the way to his residence.

As soldiers and officers dispersed, Julien went to see Zainab. He held her tightly to his chest, kissed her, and told her about the horrors he had encountered. Then he presented her with an expensive ring that he had purchased and asked her to marry him. Her eyes teared up with joy and delight as he put the ring on her finger. She asked him to do what the Egyptians do and come to her house to ask to marry her, she explained that it was not appropriate for an Egyptian woman to go through marriage by herself, he had to go to her guardian to ask for permission to marry her, she explained the guardian was the father or the guardian could be the brother if the father was absent, and since her father was deceased, he must ask her brother Ahmed for permission to marry her. She reassured him that Ahmed knew everything about him and that he would welcome him.

In the evening, Julien sat with his friends around the table waiting for dinner and told them of his plans for marriage to Zainab. She wanted an Islamic Egyptian marriage, and it would be at her home, but she did not mind a non-religious marriage if they went to France later. She was like him in that she was not a religious person and did not practice her religion, but she had a loyalty to her religion that she could not abandon. Both yearned for marriage and did not care how it was accomplished. Love overcomes all barriers. He left the marriage arrangements to Zainab, as she knew what to do.

Then the friends' conversation touched on the Levant campaign. They had yet to learn the facts because all they received was unreliable and conflicting news. Julien went on to tell them about what he witnessed in the long and arduous journey that he participated in, and all its events from Suez to Arish to Gaza, Jaffa, Acre, Mount Tabor and Tyre. They learned from him for the first time the truth about many of the events that they had heard, such as the horrific actions that took place after the seizure of Jaffa, the plague outbreak among the soldiers, confronting the English cannons during the siege of Acre and the victory over the Sultan's army near Mount Tabor. The discussion continued:

> 'Caffarelli's death is a great loss. He died of gangrene from a wound sustained by the English cannons that they erected in the castle during the siege of Acre.'

> 'The leader Bonaparte mourned him writing "Our universal regrets accompany General Caffarelli to the grave; the army is losing one of its bravest leaders, Egypt one of its greatest legislators, France one of its best citizens, and science, an illustrious scholar."'

> 'The British did more to thwart this campaign than just supporting al-Gezzar Pasha during the siege of Acre, they were the ones who persuaded the Christians in Lebanon and Syria not to cooperate with Bonaparte. They also spread many exaggerated rumours about the killing of prisoners and plague patients and stories about the death of Commander Bonaparte and the dispersion of the army. Many Egyptians believed these rumours.'

'The condition of fifteen soldiers infected with the plague had deteriorated and they were about to die, so they were given an overdose of morphine as an act of mercy. As for the injured, Commander Bonaparte was able to evacuate most of them to the army hospital in Cairo.'

'The morphine hastened their death but eased their pain and saved them from being brutally slaughtered if the Turks had found them.'

'This is exactly what the Turks did with some of the French wounded who could not be transported because of the gravity of their injuries. They were left in the Armenian monastery hospital, and the Turks came and brutally slaughtered all of them and expelled the monks from the monastery after they had been there for many centuries.'

'The Turks do not know European values. Al-Gezzar Pasha executed four hundred Christians by stitching them into cloth bags and throwing them into the sea.'

'Bonaparte was even more admired when he visited plague patients at the Armenian monastery hospital by the seaside. He picked up one of the patients himself and put him to bed.'

'Bonaparte returned on foot, like all healthy soldiers and officers, because he had ordered that horses were only for the wounded. We had to bury the cannons in the sand or throw them into the sea.'

Everyone left the restaurant and Julien remained alone as Zainab was still inside. Since he returned from fighting in the Levant he was overwhelmed with low-spirited, gloomy feelings and loneliness followed the many grave events he had seen. He wished that he could hug Zainab tightly and kiss her and then take her all for himself, but she would not allow this before she was ready for it. He knew he must wait for the right time, and then he heard her calling him from behind the door:

'I want something from you.'

'What do you want?'

She came and held his hand with both hands and pressed it hard and said:

'I want you, I want to take you now, and if you don't agree I'll take you against your will.'

He was stunned with surprise and before he could say anything, she continued:

'Hold me to your chest now, hold me tightly, I want to feel the warmth of your body and the charm of your breath. Kiss me now.'

It didn't take anything more for the volcano of love and desire inside him to erupt and burst, the two bodies stuck together and united in an overwhelming ecstasy that flew them away from this world. Time passed quickly in their frantic desire to satisfy everything their bodies desired and longed for, until they climaxed together.

Their breathing calmed and the bodies relaxed, and they were overwhelmed by a flood of happiness, comfort and peace, lying in bed with pillows scattered around them and a glass of wine with some peeled pistachios, Julien looked over to see Zainab looking at him with an absent-minded expression as if she hadn't yet woken up from a beautiful dream.

'Your virginity didn't surprise me.'

'I was a virgin, you cunning mongoose. How did you do that to me? I'm infatuated with you. You've taken away my mind. I've become your captive. Don't go away and leave me alone again.'

'I have seen too many horrors, but with you, those horrors are swiftly erased. I looked at the lucidity of your eyes and the darkness, anguish and desolation all went away.'

The next day, the marriage ceremony took place in Zainab's house. Only Julien's friends and a few of Zainab's neighbours and friends attended. Ahmed was completely unable to move, but Ali and his wife sat him comfortably among the pillows with a wide smile of satisfaction on his face. The house was filled with laughter and zaghareed, that high-tone cry of loud and lengthy cheering, that Egyptians are known for, then everyone left, and Zainab became Julien's wife.

Al-Husseiniya and al-Azbakeya district, Cairo

Feverish and painful thoughts had been circulating in Hussein's head since early morning. He had learned that this infidel French officer would marry Zainab. Such a corrupt man couldn't be left to desecrate the purity of his beloved, so he must move quickly to prevent this and kill the infidel. He felt a bit tired, dizzy, and nauseous while working in the workshop during the day, he did not know any reason for feeling a lack of strength. Nevertheless, he brought a sharp dagger from the weapons they had hidden in preparation for the day of jihad, and he put it in his belt where it could not be seen. He was determined and did not care or think about the consequences. He then took his donkey and went on his way to al-Azbakeya. He had seen the French officer before from a distance and knew that he was tall and burly, so he decided to wait until the man was alone and then surprise him from behind and cut his throat.

When he arrived at al-Azbakeya and waited on a nearby street where the French officers lived, he noticed that he was getting weaker and weaker, and his feeling of dizziness and drowsiness had significantly worsened. He felt very ill, and his strength had failed him and the desire for revenge vanished. He had no option but to go back, and so he turned around to return home and suddenly, from nowhere, he found himself face-to-face with Zainab. She too was returning home with some women. He looked at her stunning unveiled face when she said:

> 'Is this you, Hussein, what brought you to this place?'

He couldn't find anything to say, so she continued:

> 'I am a married woman now and what about you, have you married?'

> 'Yes'

> 'I would very much like to know who your wife is.'

> 'She is Suoad al-Barawi.'

> 'Is she Suoad the daughter of al-Barawi, the grain merchant?'

> 'Yes, she is, do you know her?'

> 'I know her well from childhood and I also know al-Barawi as well, because I buy wheat, corn, and beans from him. He treats me with kindness out of respect for the memory of my father, rather than estranging himself from me as did my neighbours in al-Husseiniya.'

Julien passed in front of them and stopped to find out what was the matter, Hussein stared at his face as he saw him up close for the first time. Zainab continued to speak in Arabic:

> 'This is Julien, my husband, and this is Hussein, our neighbour in al-Husseiniya.'

To his surprise, Julien replied in proper Arabic and with a friendly smile:

'Nice to meet you, Mr Hussein. Please excuse me I have to go.'

Everyone turned around and went on their way, but before she went, Zainab said in a low voice that only Hussein could hear:

'Suoad is a good girl. Do not break her heart as you broke mine.'

They left him alone. His face was hit by the cold evening breeze as he was overcome by weakness. He struggled to reach his donkey which took him back to al-Husseiniya. Weakness and faintness were increasing, thoughts were spinning in his mind, and the disease had doubled his sense of confusion, muddle and bewilderment. His feelings had changed now, and he didn't know where his thoughts would lead him. Feeling even dizzier and suffering from nausea and pains in different parts of his body, he wanted nothing more than to be able to get home and rest in bed.

In the mosque, everyone noticed that Hussein was absent from prayer, and Sheikh Abd al-Rahman said to them after the evening lesson:

'Our brother in jihad Hussein is sick, so I pray for him to heal and the best that could heal is in the

Book of God Almighty, and we have been strengthened and guided by the Prophet, peace and blessings of Allah be upon him, in saying, "Take away the hardship you the mighty Lord of the people and heal, you the healer. There is no healing except your healing, a healing that does not leave sickness." But beware of spreading the news about Hussein's illness because the infidel Francees lie in wait to take patients away to their quarantine.'

Everyone shared the call to God for healing, and then they left and started talking on the way:

'The Christians went out into the Nile in boats and prepared for dissoluteness, accompanied by musical instruments and songs, and went out of their manner. They refused to act modestly and professed with all the ugliness of laughter, ridicule, and imitating Muslims. Some of them were decorated with the uniforms of the mameluke princes of Egypt, wore their weapons, and imitated them too, impersonating their words but in mockery and scorn.'

'In that night there were many obscenities and much debauchery on the river and along its coasts, and indescribable acts of immorality were committed. The mob and common people followed the paths of lewdness and wickedness without anyone objecting to their obscenities, instead allowing everyone to do whatever they desired and came into their mind.'

Boulaq and Old Cairo district, Cairo

Happiness spread among the Christians of Cairo because of the return of Bonaparte and his army from the Levant after defeating the Sultan's army, so the danger of further war, death, and destruction in Cairo appeared to have passed. It was a time to observe the festival of the Nile, which celebrated its annual flooding. It was a day when hearts were filled with joy. People, Christians, and Muslims, went out that night to Boulaq and Old Cairo and al-Rawda and they went out into the river on boats accompanied by instruments and songs. They brought their women and the French brought more boats decorated with colourful flags and ribbons, with many types of drums and flutes playing. They also fired cannons and rockets from the boats and shores all night and carried on beating drums and playing flutes until dawn.

In the morning, Deputy Sari Askar Dugua was accompanied by the senior French officers and the elders and notable people of Egypt to the palace of the dam. They sat in it, and the soldiers lined up in the land of al-Rhoda Nile island and the land of Old Cairo district with their weapons and drums and some of them in boats fired their cannons in succession until the dam broke and the water ran into the Gulf Then they left and everyone was full of peace, joy, and elation.

The church

The church was full of people celebrating the feast of the apostles Peter and Paul. The Coptic Church commemorates the martyrdom of these two saints by the Roman Emperor Nero while they preached Christianity. Some Copts break their fast at this celebration after fasting for more than a month. Priest Athanasius went on to say Mass and the Rite of al-Lakkan and concluded by saying "Heavenly Son, you who have called the Apostles Peter and Paul and given them the power and courage to bear witness to you, give us of your

Spirit that we may overcome ourselves and live our Christianity sincerely and faithfully, that the Father, the Son and the Holy Spirit may glorify in us, forever, amen."

Christians finally felt stability and security after long months of unrest and violence. There were no further attacks on them or their property, and Bonaparte's victory over the Sultan's army in the Levant gave them some reassurance as they feared the attack of al-Ja'idiya if Bonaparte had been killed and his army dispersed as rumoured. Many felt freer than ever under the French as they could show their joy in public, wear luxurious clothes, and ride horses and mules just like Muslims.

It happened in July 1799

Al-Azbakeya district, Cairo

In al-Azbakeya Palace, the young commander Napoleon Bonaparte stood alone on the balcony of the vast Great Palace at dusk, looking at the Nile, the island, and the rare ornamental trees and shrubs in the palace's spacious garden. A man needed to be alone sometimes to reflect, think, and review events. Conflicting feelings revolved in his imagination, after the destruction of his fleet in Abu Qir he faced this other setback. He returned from the Levant without achieving his goals, having lost twelve hundred men in combat and six hundred to the plague, as well as suffering eighteen hundred more wounded. After his withdrawal following the failure the siege the Acre, the British and the Ottomans were able to regain all the lands in the Levant that he had won for France, and the British gained much for their propaganda war by spreading the news that he had executed thousands of prisoners of war and killed his own plague-ridden soldiers when the fact was that he only ordered an overdose of morphine for a few plague patients as an act of mercy. Since they were at a late stage of the disease and on their way to death, the morphine was a way to rid them of the pain and save them from brutal slaughter if they were left behind to be captured by the Turks.

After returning from the Levant, he achieved a brilliant victory against the Ottomans in Abu Qir, as he destroyed the anticipated Sultan's army that came by the sea. This not only removed the Turkish threat to Egypt but also raised the morale of his soldiers. He had paraded the Turkish prisoners in front of the Egyptians in Cairo as well. But the harsh truth remained that his dreams of an empire in the East, achieved by capturing Ottomans' land and marching towards India like Alexander the Great had ended, at least for the time being. The death of General Maximilian Caffarelli from injuries sustained during the siege of Acre was a heavy loss for his campaign and for France. He would have achieved all his goals had it not been for the plague epidemic and Sidney Smith's intervention. Again, he tasted the bitterness of defeat.

During the siege of Acre, he knew about the difficult situation back home in France from copies of European newspapers and it became clear to him that it was impossible for him to get any aid from France to support him in Egypt. He had done a lot to change and improve life in Egypt, but the Egyptians did not accept French civilization and did not understand the great reforms he had introduced to the country. There was no longer anything he could do in Egypt, and so he had to leave his duties there to others, as his ambitions and hopes were greater than just this campaign, and his great destiny had not yet been fulfilled. His presence in Egypt left him unable to proceed with his plans which was a waste of his professionalism and excellence. He would now return to France and recover what revolutionary France had lost to the allies, restore French superiority, and defend the principles of the revolution again.

However, there was some good fortune. while he was strengthening the defenses of the Citadel of Qaitbay in Rosetta, Pierre Francois Bouchard, an officer who had contact with the Scientific Institute, found a large stone of black granite with writing in three languages. Bouchard expected that a single text had been written in the three different languages, and so he informed General Menou, who told him to send the stone immediately to Cairo. Bonaparte went to see it for himself. The discovery of the stone caused a great deal of excitement and anticipation as one of these languages was that of ancient Egypt, the same that was written on the walls of the temples and that told the names and history of the kings who built them. No one, not even the Egyptians, knew how to decipher this writing. And one of the three languages on the stone was Ancient Greek, which was well known to French scholars, so it would be now possible to decipher the ancient Egyptian language, and it might be possible to read the writings on the walls of temples. He longed to know the history of the ancient Egyptian civilization, which was the basis of all others. He also longed to know how this great civilization collapsed leaving the Egyptians, once the giants of civilization, as slaves to a long series of occupiers over the centuries.

His friend Vivant Denon returned from his long journey in Upper Egypt and the Red Sea and presented to the Scientific Institute and Napoleon all the antiquities, papyrus, and drawings of temples and monuments he had brought with him. Bonaparte regretted very much that he did not have the opportunity to see the great temples and tombs in Upper Egypt himself, as he wished to do so. The most interesting was a drawing of the Zodiac of Dendera, through which they might be able to date the construction of the temple of Dendera, allowing the world to know for the first time when this ancient civilization had thrived. Indeed, France would offer the world many treasures of knowledge from what they found in Egypt.

In Zainab's house in al-Azbakeya, Zainab trembled when she returned home to see her brother Ahmed's head falling on his chest and his loyal dog licking his face. She hurried to him and raised his head, only to see the pallor of death in his face, the lack of sparkle in his eyes, and to feel the coldness of his body. Ahmed was dead. Once again death took hold of someone beloved to her.

The situation was unbearable, and she was overwhelmed with anguish and pain. She had expected it to happen at any time and prepared herself to face it when it did, but even still she wasn't truly prepared for it. She felt as if she was falling into a deep abyss of gloom, sadness and sorrow. With a detached and emotionless face, she asked Ali to bring Julien, who hurried to her. Her silence and distant eyes concerned him, but when he pressed her hands and hugged her tightly to his chest, she burst into tears. He said:

'Cry, shed all your tears, don't hold your feelings in, nothing like tears in easing sadness and binging relief, don't take on yourself what you can't bear.'

Zainab continued weeping and sobbing in his arms and he then said:

'You can't blame yourself; you did everything anyone could do facing an incurable disease. You were faithful to the memory of your father and did not let him down. Ahmed lived his short life in the best manner possible.'

He held her firmly to his chest as she sobbed. She found great comfort with her head on his shoulder and solace in his words.

Ali told the neighbours and friends, and the house became full of mourners and wailing women. Zainab sat among the mourners, and Julian's words helped her to regain control over her feelings. She knew then what to do, she had seen it repeatedly with her father and mother and then Badriya, it was the journey of separation and of no return. May Ahmad find peace and comfort between her father and mother in the afterlife. Life goes on, she thought, she would very much miss seeing Ahmed's smiling face every evening, but she wouldn't be alone, and her life now had a new meaning with Julien by her side.

Al-Husseiniya district, Cairo

Hussein woke up late in the morning exhausted and weakened, unable to leave his bed and showing fever and sickness. Suoad called for help from his mother, who hurried with the servants to bring some herbal medicines, and Haj Ibrahim in a rush brought home a healer to examine his son.

Concern appeared on the face of the healer who advised them of the need to inform the Sheikh of the neighborhood. According to the letter the French had displayed on the markets and lanes about the plague, the healer advised Haj Ibrahim that he must inform the sheikh because otherwise he would be fined and flogged and possibly face the death penalty, he also explained that the French would not tolerate any slackness in this reporting and they would not listen to the intercession of the sheikhs in this regard.

Immediately the healer informed the Sheikh of the neighbourhood, who told the French governor of the district who immediately passed it on to the deputy governor of the town. It was not long before a French doctor came with a number of male nurses and after examining Hussein confirmed that he was infected with the plague and ordered him to be taken to quarantine in al-Rawda. Hussein saw what was happening around him in a state of weakness and muddle and found it difficult to speak, unable to do anything. They took Hussein from his house amid the cries, screams and entreaties of his wife and mother and the crying of his siblings while his bewildered father wouldn't stop repeating supplications and reciting verses from the Quran: "God does not burden a soul beyond its ability to cope", "My God ease my hardship with your authority and power and remove my anguish with your kindness and mercy", "we worship you and from you, we seek help."

Then French soldiers came and surrounded the house and warned that no one could enter or leave Haj Ibrahim's house for four days and they took Hussein's clothes and burned them and warned that the house had to be guarded all the time. If anyone passed and touched the door, they would arrest them and put them in quarantine inside the house with the others.

Al-Rawda Island, Cairo

After the doctor's examination, they isolated Hussein from the rest of the family and took him from his home to the French Hospital for plague patients on the Nile Island of al-Rawda. They put him to bed in a room full of other patients. He had no strength and was exhausted, and he felt dizzy, drowsy, and sleepy as he surrendered to his fate, unable to resist or argue, watching what was happening around him in silence. Doctors and nurses in bizarre uniforms were all around, and the other patients were covered with swellings, abscesses, blisters and leaking pus, mucus and blood, he watched as they took the dead away and replaced them with new patients quite frequently.

Within two days, Hussein's body was also covered with swellings in the armpit, groin and neck then these places turned into abscesses and blisters and started leaking pus and mucus and blood as he saw happening to others around him. He knew that in a day or two parts of his body would turn black as it happened to others, the Black Death was coming to him, and he was not even able to recite the Quran or utter a word, so he kept repeating in his mind the two Islamic testimonies "I bear witness that there is no god but Allah and I bear witness that Muhammad is the Messenger of God." He asked God for forgiveness and mercy, and kept reciting in his mind other verses from the Quran; "Your Lord is broad in forgiveness, he knows you best, as He raised you from the earth and when you are embryos in the wombs of your mothers", "Oh God, I ask you for forgiveness, Oh God, cover our nakedness and relief our fears", "your Lord is forgiving and merciful", "the forgiving and welcoming". Then he fell into a coma and the faces of his mother, Zainab, and Suoad appeared to him. He was confused and fearful between them and that tormented him, but as time passed, he felt that he was no longer frightened or tormented and his anxiety faded as he looked at their faces without any feelings and he felt peace. Everything began to slip away and the world around him was vanishing, then he fell into an infinitely deep abyss of loss, darkness, and silence.

Days passed, he didn't know how many, before Hussein opened his eyes not knowing where he was. In front of him was the face of the French doctor smiling and speaking to him in French and a little bit of Arabic. Next to him an interpreter said:

> 'The French doctors have treated you until you were cured.'

And then he translated the doctor's words:

'You were lucky, Mr Hussein, you survived the Black Death. We know that out of every ten patients, nine inevitably die, and you were one of the few who have recovered from this disease. We will now let you go.'

He was weak in body and mind feeling as if what was happening around him was a dream and not a reality. They took him out of the hospital to find his father and a large crowd of people waiting for him and took him on the long journey to his home in al-Husseiniya, where he found another crowd waiting for him with shouting, cheering, singing, and zaghareed and shaking tambourines and banging drums. He noticed Souad's face making zahgareed and laughing in the middle of the noise and crowd. His father held a huge dinner feast in celebration and distributed alms and handouts to the poor all over the neighbourhood. Hussein looked around and smiled at those present. Finally, everyone left him to go to bed and rest with Suoad next to him, he then felt her warm tears as she kissed his hands and then went to sleep close to him.

Al-Hussainiyah district, Cairo

Sheikh Abd al-Rahman viewed the recent events with pronounced sorrow. The great Sari Askar crossed the river Nile to Giza with thousands of French soldiers following him. He did not announce the reason for this, and people were amazed, but then it turned out to be that he was on his way to face the Sultan's army that came by sea at Alexandria. The Sultan's army first came to Abu Qir, seized the castle, and killed all the French. When this news reached Cairo, the Cairene Muslims showed their pleasure and delight and openly cursed the Christians. Then the news came that the Muslims and the Ottoman military had taken Alexandria, so more joy spread among Muslims and fear among Christians. This did not last long, as the joy vanished when the news arrived that the French fought the Ottoman soldiers and defeated them. They had killed many of them, seized tremendous amounts of booty and taken many prisoners as they regained control over the castle of Abu Qir and Alexandria. They also took the commander of the army of the Sultan, Mustafa Pasha, prisoner. Then several boats arrived in Cairo with Ottoman prisoners and wounded soldiers, so the news was confirmed, and sorrow and dispiritedness replaced the pleasure and delight.

In the mosque after the prayer, Sheikh Abd al-Rahman finished a lesson in a series of hadith lessons from the books of al-Bukhari and Muslim. Hussein was still absent from both the prayers and lessons, and some talked about what happened in Abu Qir. Then Sheikh Abd al-Rahman went on to say:

'What happened in Alexandria is nothing but a punishment from God for the gravity of our sins. God is the healer of anguish and the alleviator of hardships, if he wants something he simply makes it so. God alone answers the supplications, the most merciful of this world and the hereafter, forgiving sins that cut off hope and hasten annihilation.'

'There is no god but Allah, the Great and the meek, there is no God but Allah, Lord of the Great Throne, there is no God but Allah, Lord of the heavens and Lord of the earth.'

'The Hijri year has passed with all its calamities, tribulations and horrors. There were many strange incidents that happened that were not heard of before.'

'The greatest incident was the interruption of the pilgrimage from Egypt to Mecca. Al-Kaaba clothing was not sent, something that has not happened in all these centuries or in the days of the Ottomans.'

'Hussein has recovered and left the quarantine, and soldiers have lifted the guard from Haj Ibrahim's house.'

'Allah healed him and saved him from the hands of the disbelievers and brought him back safely to his family. All this was achieved by the prayers of the believers. He will be back with us soon, God willing.'

'Everything is up to God alone.'

Al-Sanadikya district, Cairo

Sari Askar Bonaparte came back to his home in al-Azbakeya after his victory over the Sultan's army and brought with him the Muslim prisoners, so many that people went to al-Azbakeya to verify the news of a French victory which was hard to believe. They saw the Muslim prisoners standing in the middle for everyone to see, and after this display, they took the prisoners to military prisons in the

Citadel and in an unused mosque converted into a military base. The French did not bring Mustafa Pasha Sari Askar of the Ottomans, to Cairo with the other prisoners but instead sent him with honour to Giza.

The friends, as usual, always had differing views. Some were sympathetic to the French, some were hostile, and some took a view in between. But they were brought together by laughter, giggles, cups of coffee and shisha. They all cordially shared their delight and joy for the return of Hussein to his home and the lifting of the guards around the house of his father Haj Ibrahim. Their chatter continued:

> 'They took Hussein into quarantine, and his news was cut off from us. It was only by the generosity of God that he was healed and returned to us healthy, but if they took a patient and he died, his family would never see him again and they would not know anything about him, the undertakers would take him with his cloths and bury him in a deep grave in a distant graveyard.'
>
> 'God's generosity was behind Hussein's cure.'
>
> 'Healing is from God.'
>
> 'The plague occurred in Egypt but did not spread in the neighbourhood because of the French

preparations to prevent it. They called for keeping clothes and bedding in the washing lines on the roofs for several days and for fumigating houses with incense to stop mouldiness. They also ordered the sheikhs of the neighbourhoods, the governors and the police to inspect and search homes for the sick and for neglect. They appointed a woman and two men in each neighbourhood to enter the houses to check for these things, so the woman goes up to the top of the house and tells them about the validity of their deployment then they go after checking and call on the people of the house to follow the rules and warn against neglect, all that to get rid of rot that brings the plague. They issued proclamations about these measures and put them on the walls of the markets and lanes as they used to do.'

'They warned people not to bury the dead in graveyards near their dwellings and instead to use only graveyards far away from their homes and to dig the graves deep. People must inform of any sick person so they could send a French doctor to see if the disease was the plague. People must also inform about the dead.'

'One of the French arrangements that prevented the plague was that if a person died in his home and it appeared that he was plagued, they collected all his clothes and bedding and burned them. Only undertakers were allowed to handle the body, and they were buried without a funeral and in front of him were guards to prevent passers-by from approaching the diseased body, and if someone did anyway they took him to be quarantined with the undertakers.'

'The commoners did not take the French arrangements on the basis that they prevented the spread of the plague, they despised and hated them, and many began to flee Cairo to the countryside.'

'The ships came to Alexandria with the army of the Sultan, some were from the kingdom of the Moskov who worship three gods.'

'This is a lie and slander to deceive Muslims, it is one of Bonabarta's tricks with the aim of making people hate the Sultan.'

'The Moskov are Orthodox Christians like us, the Greek Orthodox, they worship one God, not three gods, and we say that this one God has three hypostases, but we believe in one god like you Muslims.'

'And what about the Copts?'

'Copts also believe in one God with three hypostases, but they consider us deviant from the upright faith.'

'You Greek Orthodox also consider the Copts to be deviant from the upright faith.'

Everyone laughed and the conversation continued:

'Bonabarta said to the sheikhs and notables who came and greeted him that when he travelled to the Levant they were on good behaviour in his absence. But this time, they were not, as they thought the Franks would not return but die and parish. They were happy and optimistic about this, and he also said that he was amazed by their sadness for the French victory, even so, bonabarta had declared to them that he believed that there was no god but Allah and that he adored the prophet and loved the Muslims. The sheikhs denied their sadness for his victory and said this was not the case.'

'They celebrated the prophet's birthday festival in al-Azbakeya and Sheikh Khalil al-Bakri invited the great Sari Askar and a group of French notables to have dinner with him. They fired cannons and rockets and they called for decorations and opened the markets and shops, which were decorated with so many lamps it looked like a carnival.'

The church:

In the evening, Father Athanasius was kneeling in the church alone in an individual prayer to God, asking Him to protect the church and the Coptic congregation. He prayed in the Coptic language as he felt that the Lord heard prayers more in Coptic and regretted very much that the congregation could no longer speak the language, even though it was the language used in Mass every week. He concluded his prayer by saying, Lord Jesus, you who said, "Come to me, you who labour and are heavily laden, and I will give you rest", behold, I come to you and put before you all the burdens of my life, for I believe that you will bear them from me today and every day, as you once carried the cross, and wash away sins with your gracious blood.

Then he went to his bedroom alone to sleep, filled with comfort, tranquillity, and peace. The danger of al-Ja'idiya's attacks on the church receded when the news arrived of Bonabarta's victory in Abu Qir. He did not see any harassment from the French, they spoke to him kindly, but they had no religion, and their ideology corrupted the minds of Mu'allim Yaqub and his associates and followers.

It happened in August 1799

The Mediterranean Sea near the African coast:

Napoleon Bonaparte lay in his cabin on the frigate Muiron suffering a bit from seasickness while one of his assistants was reading him a history book about the Englishman Oliver Cromwell.

He was now on the way to France. He prepared the frigates Muiron and Carrier for a secret mission unknown to even his closest generals. It seemed to everyone that these two ships would carry a number of the expedition's scientists back to the French Scientific Institute along with of with the antiquities and scientific samples that they took from Egypt. But in fact, the plan was for Bonaparte to leave with them. The English fleet was enforcing a tight siege on the Egyptian shores but somehow, Bonaparte was able to outmanoeuvre Sidney Smith and his spies and sailed secretly from a small port nine miles away from Alexandria. On this day, the wind helped him to escape quickly and sail parallel to the coast of Africa on the way to Corsica and from there to Paris.

Reflecting on the recent events; It was unwise for Bonaparte to remain in Egypt while France faced the threat of invasion from Russia, Austria and Britain. The Republic could not face this danger while its greatest general was far away in Egypt. After the elimination of the Turkish invasion army at Abu Qir, the threat to Egypt receded and it became safe to leave the army under the command of Kleber, as Bonaparte now had more important tasks in France.

He was fairly certain of Egypt's stability and the leadership of Kleber, leaving him a letter advising him to "gain the trust of senior ulema in Cairo because who earns their trust guarantees the confidence of the Egyptian people". He left another letter to the Cairo Diwan telling them that he "entrusted the leadership to General Kleber and that he is a distinguished man I am proud of. I have asked him to have the same love for the ulema and imams that I have for them. Do everything you can so that the people of Egypt have the same confidence in Kleber that they had in me. This nation will be the source of my happiness when I return in two or three months and do not make me carry anything but praise and reward to the ulema when I return."

While travelling, he spent his time between engineering, chemistry and history books, and he was completely satisfied with what had been scientifically accomplished in Egypt during that short period. Before the campaign, all that the world knew about Egypt was what a few European travellers wrote with their own limited knowledge. But in his campaign, he brought with him the most skilled scientists, artists and craftsmen in France-engineers, technicians, astronomers, architects, chemists, scientists in natural history and metallurgy, painters, musicians, poets and orientalists, so that the world would know a lot about Egypt and enrich the civilization and science for all humanity.

Al-Azbakeya district, Cairo

General Kleber was outraged to learn of Bonaparte's departure. How dare the Corsican runt do this? Bonaparte abandoned his army and his mistress Pauline and was gone. Couldn't Bonaparte find the courtesy to discuss it with Kleber before he went? Bonaparte ordered Kleber to meet in Rashid and then surprised him with this letter informing him of his departure from Egypt on his way to France and assigning him to lead the army in Egypt. General Kleber now faced a grave responsibility for which no one envied him. The British, Turks and Mamelukes are preparing for a new offensive and his forces were exhausted by the plague and the losses suffered during the campaign in the Levant.

He quickly regained his usual calm and poise and discussed these new developments at al-Azbakeya Palace with his generals. He read Napoleon Bonaparte's letter to them in which he said that the Directory had summoned him, that he was in great pain to go, that he had difficulty leaving his army to which he had been so closely attached, that he would arrange for support troops from France to be sent to strengthen the expeditionary army and that he would eventually return to Egypt. Kleber read all of this, but within his heart, he knew that the Republic was facing the threat of invasion from the Allies and that it was impossible to send support forces at the time. He explained to his generals that he would seek a peace treaty with the English and Turks to ensure an honourable withdrawal of troops and a return to France and tasked General Desaix to begin negotiations with the Englishman Sidney Smith on the matter. He knew that his generals, officers, and soldiers were desperate to return home. Bonaparte's sudden departure could have caused protest and rebellion, but Kleber, for whom everyone had the utmost respect and trust, handled it in a way to that maintained calm.

Al-Sanadikya district, Cairo

The Friends sat in the garden of Haj Mustafa's house. They liked to stay up late on summer nights. The sudden departure of Sari Askar the Great to France caused them a lot of confusion, they received the news of Bonabarta's letter to the people of Egypt brought by the deputy Dugua saying that he left to travel to the French country on Friday the 21st of the month for the comfort of the people of Egypt and to open the sea route and he would be absent for about three months and then return to remove the corrupt away. Then the letter mentioned the leadership of the people of Egypt and the leadership of the French during his absence was handed to Kleber the Sari Askar of Damietta.

The friends talked about how the new Sari Askar the great Kleber had come to Cairo and they celebrated his arrival by firing cannons from all the castles. He was received by all the French seniors and juniors then he moved to the house where Bonabarta lived which was previously the house of al-Alfi Bey in al-Azbakia and lived in his place. The country's elders from the ulemas and notables went to meet the new Sari Askar to greet him but were surprised that he did not meet them that day and promised to meet them the next. When they attended on the second day, they did not receive a warm welcome or feel any cheerfulness from him as they used to see from Bonaparte, who was nice, and humble and laughed with them.

Everyone wondered what the new French prince Kleber would be like. While Mansour sat among them, his thoughts were spinning in his head. Despite the recent defeat, the people were still waiting for the Sultan's army to rid them of the Franks. Mansour knew that the Mameluke princes and the Ottomans couldn't confront the French with their modern methods of warfare. It had now become clear to him that only the English had enough superiority in fighting methods to defeat them, and that the Sultan, with all his greatness, had sought their help. If al-Alfi could join them, then he could return victorious and restore sovereignty to the princes again. Mansour could then regain the same power and influence under the command of al-Alfi Bey as he had under the command of Murad Bey.

The rumbling of shisha and the sounds of coffee and cinnamon sipping interrupted their talking:

'People were puzzled and wondered how Bonabarta managed to leave and sail across the sea in the presence of the English Navy boats and their siege of the ports all the time summer and winter since their arrival in Egypt.'

'No one knows how he escaped and went; he is good at tricks and is very cunning.'

'We don't know what things will be like after Bonabarta who did not do anything that offended Islam, did not take sides with Christians, and always showed respect for Islam and for the ulemas. They considered him an infidel, but they found pleasure in provoking religious discussions in his presence, and they admired him very much for his mighty brain, which made them secretly believe that he would join them one day in raising the banner of Islam.'

'That sullen-faced new Sari Askar ordered the Coptic Christians to collect one hundred- and fifty-thousand-riyal fransah and they went ahead to collect it.'

'The new Sari Askar showed the Egyptians that he was the king and he reigned as he rode from al-Azbakeya into the city centre in a magnificent procession until he went up to the Citadel. In front of him were about five hundred workers with canes in their hands ordering people to get up and stand for his passage and he was accompanied by many of the Francees cavalry and in their hands they carried drawn swords. With them rode the governors and other leaders and Barttalmin, as well as the constabularies and deputies and their followers in the parade. When he went up to the castle they fired several cannons, and he inspected it and then he went down with that procession to his house.'

'They did not ask the sheikhs, the heads of the Diwan, to attend him or to walk in that procession. The new Sari Askar approached them with gentleness as Bonabarta did, and he visited the house of the Chief of the Diwan, Sheikh Abdullah al-Sharqawi. The sheikh received him and held a great feast at his home and invited notables, merchants and other sheikhs to have dinner with him.'

'As Bonabarta used to do, the new Sari Askar went to the house of Sheikh Sadat late in the afternoon with many of the Francees' notables and that was at the end of the birth of Husseini festival. They travelled in a great procession and in front of them was the governor, the deputies, a body of constables and a large number of their soldiers and with drawn swords in their hands. They dinned there and rode back after sunset and saw the lighting of the lamps.'

'The ulema and notables only pretended to receive him in welcome.'

The Church

Father Athanasius held a daily mass in his church for two weeks during the Lent of the Virgin Mary. After Mass on the last day of Lent, many relatives and friends gathered at the house of Saadallah, who used to hold a large feast of iftar and a celebration of the feast of the Virgin. After abstaining from eating meat and all animal products during Lent, they were served Fattah, a stew made with rice and roasted bread surrounded by all kinds of grilled and roasted meat, and meat cooked with vegetables.

The Copts are so keen on following the Lent of the Virgin Mary, some of them cook with water and salt but no oil and they eat Doqqa and Shallawlaw during this period. Many people do an extra week of Lent, not only because the Virgin has visited and blessed Egypt, but also because of the many miracles that occurred through the intercession of the Virgin.

The women sat with the children on one side while the men sat together on the other side, talking:

> 'Bonabarta had little confidence in the Copts, seeking to strip them of the work that they did for centuries. He wanted a new tax system that would allow him to dispense with the Copts' services.'
>
> 'Bonabarta had regard for Muslims and not for Copts, no one knows what the new Sari Askar would be like with the Copts.'
>
> 'The Francees are full of the spirit of justice and equality. Even if they showed an inclination towards Islam in front of Muslims, they did not fail to protect Christians.'

'Although the Copts did not welcome the French and during the revolution considered themselves in solidarity with their Muslim compatriots, many members of the public imagine the Copts to be happy for the French and gloating over the suffering of the Muslims.'

'The presence of the French caused us difficulties with the Muslims, and we are afraid that we will be subjected to Muslim revenge if the French leave.'

'Mu'allim Yaqub's wealth grew and his influence increased, which also caused us difficulties with the Muslims.'

'Our master the Patriarch is not satisfied with his actions and behaviour, Mu'allim Yaqub deviated from the laws of the Church and took a non-Coptic woman as a wife, and in dress and demeanour he violates our Coptic traditions.'

Al-Husseiniya district, Cairo

Hussein sat eating breakfast in the morning before going to work; Suoad did not share breakfast with him but served him, making sure to please him, and then took her breakfast with his mother later. He prayed al-Fajr prayer in congregation in the mosque whenever he could and noticed that Suoad, as ever, never missed al-Fajr prayers. She followed all the fundamental practices of Islam, repeated litanies, and had never appeared in public without her veil since childhood; she fulfilled all his demands and sometimes fulfilled his requests before he asked. She obeyed his mother in everything, and his mother loved her as her daughter. She was like his mother, often repeating loudly her thanks to God for his recovery from the deadly plague. Like his mother, she visited and fulfilled her many vows to the tombs of righteous Muslim sheikhs and the pieties and talked often about their numerous miracles. He used to consider that a heresy, but it no longer made him angry with her. Many in his family loved Sufism - the songs, rituals and doctrines - and this nostalgia had returned to him. He started talking to Suoad a lot, spending time with her, and not treating her as harshly as he used to. He noticed joy and delight in her face when he talked to her nicely. What a humble, meek and gentle girl she was. She really was a good girl.

Hussein prayed with his peers in the mosque and attended Sheikh Abd al-Rahman's lessons with them, but he left afterward and did not participate in their conversations after the lesson as he used to do. Sheikh Abd al-Rahman noticed this change and knew that his father was a Sufi and predicted that his recent illness would have made him nostalgic for Sufism again after he had moved away from it since he enrolled in his lessons in the mosque.

After the prayer, Sheikh Abd al-Rahman asked Hussein to wait, spoke to him alone, and asked if he would go with his father to Sufi Zikr. Hussein answered in the affirmative and said that he just liked to praise the greatness and glory of God and liked the spirituality of it. Sheikh Abd al-Rahman's voice changed, showing that he was unsatisfied with what Hussein was doing. Sufism was the result of Shiism, he said, deviance from true Islam, and there was no legal basis for Sufism in the Qur'an or the Sunnah. It came from Indian, Greek and Persian sources and was never Arabic. Sheikh Abd al-Rahman went on to say that Sufis spread heresies and acts that were forbidden and utterly contrary to the provisions of Sharia and the texts of the Qur'an and Sunnah.

On the shore of the Nile

Zainab and Julien stood on the shore of the Nile in the late afternoon with their hands clasped together. It was the same secluded place behind dense prickly pear bushes where they had met before when Zainab's heart beat with love for the first time. Both wanted to go back to the same place. Zainab brought a dinner prepared by her most skilled chef and decided they would eat together on the Nile shore and watch the sunset before returning home. Recovering sweet memories returns joy to the soul. They sat down together to eat by the river and exchanged chatter and laughter. The splendour and richness of the place made them not think about the world and what was happening in it- the conflicts, wars, unrest, and miseries. Instead, they sat on the shore of the Nile, talking lovers' talk. The sound of flowing water, sparrows chirping, glory and magic in trees, palms and flowers evoked in them feelings of love and a sense of tranquillity and peace.

Julien took off his clothes and went down to bathe in the Nile, and Zainab followed him into the water, so he pursued her, and their loud laughter echoed across the water. They came out of the water and sat next to each other on the beach; the sun disk in front of them was slowly creeping towards the distant horizon, daylight was fading, and the singing of the curlew began. When these rewinding tweets came from afar, the spirit flew into the sky, and the angels played on their heartstrings. They shared an hour of serenity and peacefulness of soul that is rarely found at a time when the world around them was full of violence, pain, and tears. They wished they could stay in this place until the end of the world. Zainab said:

> 'No one knows about this remote place; no one comes here. We own this place no one shares with us; let's do whatever we want; let's spend the night here.'

They lay on the river's shore, and their two bodies touched, united, and gained happiness and ecstasy; then the breaths calmed down, and they rested together in a quiet and pleasant sleep as if they were in a fantasy world away from this world and all its events. They woke up together before dawn and sat in silence. The sun disappears every day behind the horizon, and the universe becomes gloomy and dark, but it always rises and shines again. They were on a date with the sunrise, and the sun is never late.

The first ray of light from afar emanated from behind the dense prickly pear bushes and their beautiful fruits. The sun moved slowly, slowly up into the sky for darkness and sadness to vanish and the universe to be filled with light and joy. Then the earth acquired its bright colours, the sunlight sparkled on bushes, trees, and palms and reflected on the waves of the Nile, dew drops fell on the leaves, sent warmth into spirits and renewed hearts with hope and the love of life.

The foxes returned to their dens; the night birds settled in their nests. Ants, bees, hoopoes, egrets, and herons woke up, each seeking his livelihood. The place was filled with sparrows chirping in charming harmony with the singing of the nightingale and the goldfinch. The sky was decorated with flocks of flying ducks and wild geese. The universe was smiling.

The hour of dawn has a charming impact on souls and fills hearts with splendour and majesty. They looked at each other in silence. It was time to go back.